## Praise for *The Imagination Warriors*...

"A delightful romp from the high-desert settings of Northern New Mexico across the limitless lands of imagination. Laws of discovery and wonder rule Romanelli's captivating world of inspired nonconformity, where an unexpected assembly of characters finds courage, connection, and friendship in the forces of art and creativity. Together they bend space and time to break the bounds of ordinary and encounter the essence of imagination. Their adventures encourage us to tap in to the fierce warrior spirit required to be an artist, an authentic individual, or a talking cat, reminding us that magic lies in the theater of an open mind."

—CARMELLA PADILLA

Author of *The Work of Art* and recipient of the 2009 New Mexico Governor's Award for Excellence in the Literary Arts

"This first children's book from Marc Romanelli—a beautifully told story with excellent illustrations—is a delightful treat for adults as well. Here, drawing on his creative abilities in photography, Romanelli has opened up an entirely new medium for his storytelling. Readers will love it!"

—CATHERINE ALLEN

Chairman and CEO, The Santa Fe Group, and author of *The Retirement Boom, Reboot Your Life,* and *The Artist's Way at Work*

"Marc Romanelli weaves a magical, fur-tingling tale that travels through time, art, and love. Journey to unexpected lands to meet brave, bold, and sometimes belligerent characters who remind us that the power of imagination is a gift and our most creative force. This is an enticing adventure for nine- to fourteen-year-olds and an engaging read-aloud for families."

—BETH A. CLAYTON

Founder and director, Journey Montessori School

"In contemporary clinical psychoanalysis, a goal is to contemplate, explore and engage multiple states of *self-experience*. With a gleeful wink and a reverent nod to Natsume Sōseki's once banned *I Am a Cat*, Marc Romanelli's adventure invites the reader—young and, alas, not so young—into a similar engagement. The ride is full of thrilling and unexpected twists and turns that have me aching for whatever's next for the characters in this heart-thumping tale. In multiple self-experience, one hopes to hold together a balance, an integrity and consistency across and within a sometimes-vast array of difference, contrast and conflict. At the center of *The Imagination Warriors*, Romanelli holds together such a balance and harmony—between reader and read, character and context, storyteller and reader. *Bravo!*"

—MARK B. BORG JR., PHD

Clinical/Community psychologist, psychoanalyst, and author of *Irrelationship and Relationship Sanity*

The Imagination Warriors

# The IMAGINATION WARRIORS

## BOOK ONE

## MARC ROMANELLI

*" Use Your Imagination !"*

Illustrated by Odessa Sawyer
Frontispiece art by David Romanelli

Little Roman Press
Lamy, New Mexico

Published by: Little Roman Press
            #6 Lamy Station Trail
            Lamy, NM 87540
            www.littleromanpress.com

Editors: Ann Mason, Ellen Kleiner
Interior design and production: Janice St. Marie

FIRST EDITION

Printed in Canada

**Publisher's Cataloging-in-Publication Data**
Names:      Romanelli, Marc, author. | Sawyer, Odessa, illustrator. |
            Romanelli, David, illustrator.
Title:      The imagination warriors / Marc Romanelli ; illustrated by
            Odessa Sawyer ; frontispiece art by David Romanelli.
Description: First edition. | Lamy, New Mexico : Little Roman Press,
            [2018] | Series: Imagination warriors ; book one. | Audience:
            ages 9-14. | Summary: A psychic tabby cat from New York
            City teams up with a feisty nine-year-old girl living in Lamy,
            New Mexico, to solve multiple mysteries involving paintings
            that serve as portals through time and space.--Publisher.
Identifiers: ISBN: 978-0-9996389-0-3 (hardcover) | 978-0-9996389-1-0
            (ebook) | LCCN: 2018902659
Subjects:   LCSH: Children--Psychic ability--Juvenile fiction. | Space
            and time--Juvenile fiction. | Time travel--Juvenile fiction. |
            Painting--Juvenile fiction. | Artists--Juvenile fiction. | Cats--
            Psychic aspects--Juvenile fiction. | CYAC: Psychic ability--
            Fiction. | Space and time--Fiction. | Time travel--Fiction. |
            Painting--Fiction. | Artists--Fiction. | Cats--Fiction. | BISAC:
            JUVENILE FICTION / Time travel. | JUVENILE FICTION /
            Science Fiction. | JUVENILE FICTION / Animals / Cats.
Classification: LCC: PZ7.1.R6678 I43 2018 | DDC: [Fic]--dc23

1  3  5  7  9  10  8  6  4  2

To all the wonderfully unbalanced, fragile, misunderstood, brilliant, and fiercely courageous artists who, throughout time, have elevated the human spirit and allowed us a glimpse, through their unique portals, into a world of transcendent possibilities

# ACKNOWLEDGMENTS

First, for generally inspiring the writing of this book I wish to especially thank the original Daisy the cat, a soulful creature who lived with my family for many years, and my daughter Philomena, who personifies the feisty independent spirit of the book's central character and the concept of imagination warriors.

I am also deeply indebted to my parents, Ralph and Antoinette Romanelli, for their unwavering support of all my endeavors as I was growing up, and to my wise wife, Ahdina, and our extraordinary son, Redford, who, along with Philomena, remain my greatest supporters and muses.

I wish to express gratitude as well to my first editor, Leah T. Brown, for helping shepherd the book in its early developmental stage; our unique village of Lamy, New Mexico, which has been fertile ground for creating scenes about temporal anomalies and curious spatial dislocations; Carmella Padilla, Sarah Stark, and Andy Dudzik for critiquing an early incarnation of the book; photographer Edward Curtis, whose iconic image of a young Native woman with a canoe at the edge of a vast body of water, seemingly about to embark on a transformative adventure, was a guiding spiritual touchstone of this book; and my in-laws, Jean and Bill, who passionately embraced my new creative direction and faithfully read all my nascent efforts at writing each chapter.

In addition, I extend heartfelt thanks to Jonathan Dixon for designing a logo that perfectly represents the spirit of this publishing company; my fiercely talented artist brother, David Romanelli, for creating the extraordinary oil painting, reminiscent of a tarot card, that graces the cover and frontispiece of the book; Odessa Sawyer for her stellar illustrations, which powerfully capture the story's inherent wonder and awe; my developmental editor, Ann Mason, whose tough love and steely clarity steered me toward making this book sing; Cathy Allen and her dedicated crew at the Reboot Your Life Workshop for encouraging this work; and finally, Ellen Kleiner and Blessingway Authors' Services for helping me strap wings on this thing to make it soar.

# CHAPTER 1

Daisy May shifted her weight on her custom purple pillow on the windowsill as she surveyed the activity below through her apartment window high above New York City. Three days of solid rain was making her little bones ache. She did not want to admit it, but she was feeling her age. She no longer felt like the spunky gray tabby kitten with boundless energy and enthusiasm she had been when adopted by Mrs. Z. Nevertheless, she could still engage in her favorite pastime—what she considered precognitive people-watching.

Looking down on the sea of black umbrellas and tiny dots bustling below her, she spotted a woman dressed in black walking fast. "Now, will she turn right or left at the crosswalk, or will she simply walk straight ahead?" Daisy May wondered. "Definitely right." As she approached the crosswalk, the woman abruptly turned her boots and umbrella to the right. Daisy May smiled to herself.

Next Daisy May spotted a pizza delivery boy running to his bicycle. "Hmm, he'll definitely turn toward 72nd," she thought. Daisy May watched as the delivery boy strapped his helmet under his chin, kicked off from the curb, and, indeed, headed toward 72nd. "Right again!" Daisy May thought, satisfied that she was still a clairvoyant cat. She was aware that, over time, she had developed strange psychic powers, which she had tried to strengthen by watching people below her. In her dreams, she was able to use her psychic powers in many ways, such as to solve great mysteries, instead of only predicting which way pedestrians would turn when she was awake. Being aware of a greater potential use of her gifts sometimes frustrated her. "There's little opportunity to use my powers in any exciting or adventurous ways while sitting high up on my pillow looking at the world passing by below," she thought.

Daisy May felt she had settled into a rather sedentary and ordinary existence. As she looked down on the Chinese restaurant, pizza parlor, nail salon, bank, and mobile phone store in her immediate vicinity, she mused, cynically, "What would we all do without cold sesame noodles, bright shiny nails, endless supplies of cash, and the ability to talk to anyone, anywhere, at any time?" Over the years, Daisy May had established a specific routine. Each day she would wake up on the twenty-second floor of the high-rise apartment on the Upper East Side of Manhattan that she shared with Mrs. Z and take her place in the panoramic bay window atop her purple pillow (a gift from Mrs. Z), open her morning paper with the help of doting Mrs. Z (usually to the entertainment and gossip pages), and then lap milk out of her ornate, beaded Turkish bowl brought back by Mrs. Z from a trip to Istanbul. After finishing, she would stare out the window and play her game of precognitive people-watching.

But she had to admit, if she was honest, that she was rather bored with the same routine day after day. She recalled how gifted and destined for greatness the woman at the animal shelter had made her feel the night she had turned up there as an abandoned kitten. She had looked up through the driving cold rain and seen the welcoming electric blue sign that read "Animal Shelter." Somehow she had known how to read the sign and that she had to enter the door under it. She had waited until somebody came along to open the door and then padded into the warm, well-lit room. "Poor kitty, you must be frozen," a kind portly woman wearing a white lab coat had whispered to her when she saw the tiny soaking gray tabby kitten with mysterious sparkly yellow eyes. She had relaxed in the woman's arms and fallen asleep. Upon waking, she was disoriented but soon realized that she had been placed in a small smelly metal box with bars that allowed her to look out at other small little metal boxes, each containing a sad animal. She had never heard such barking and meowing in her life. "Why don't they talk like me?" she had asked herself. While licking herself clean, she had pondered the possible reasons for other animals being seemingly incapable of talking. "Maybe they never learned, or maybe the older ones forgot," she had thought. As new to the world as she was, she had had a very strong feeling that she was different from other animals. The large woman in the lab coat had looked inquisitively into her little metal room and said, reassuringly, "You may be the cutest little ball of fur I've ever seen. I wish I could keep you myself, but I've got a very jealous dog at home. I just know you'll find a home soon, sweetie pie." She had looked up at the woman and decided to speak to her. In a scratchy little voice, she had proclaimed, "I am destined for a big life because I have a big spirit." Aghast, the woman had looked around the big sterile room to see if anyone was in earshot of their conversation. Then the woman had opened the cage door, scooped her up, and whispered, "You are only the second animal I've ever encountered with the gift of speech. The other is my dog. You may well be destined for greatness. Do you have a name?" After thinking about the question, she had stated definitively, "I will name myself Daisy May." The woman had placed her very gently back in her cage but had not closed its door. Then she had peered into Daisy May's eyes and said mysteriously, "I can tell that you have the gift, and I'm certain you'll find your owner before your owner finds you."

Just then a petite older woman, dressed very stylishly, had walked into the animal shelter apparently looking for something, and carrying a little straw basket with fabric lining. All the cats and dogs had begun to bark and whine, but the woman seemed not to hear them. Daisy

May had quickly said to herself with great confidence, "That is the woman who will take me home. She is kind but a little lonely." Immediately, the petite woman with the basket had turned and walked directly to her then looked into her cage, gently patted her head, and said, "You'll fit perfectly in my basket, dear one." From that day on, she had lived comfortably with Mrs. Z, who had raised her with appreciation of her special gifts.

Now, though, Daisy May's use of her gifts was limited in the apartment. She focused on the worn cover of *Desperado Gulch*. In addition to her guessing game, another favorite pastime of Daisy May's was to read the novels that Mrs. Z got for her at the local library. Currently, she was favoring pulpy western novels. There was something that fascinated her about the wide-open spaces of the West and their weathered characters with waxed moustaches living by their wits in unforgiving, harsh environments. To relieve boredom, after much trial and error she'd developed a clever technique for opening the pages of her books. She would lick a page with her tongue until it lifted a little, then push the page over with her paw. It was a tedious procedure, but it worked. She looked at the cover illustration of the rugged cowboy and his trusty steed and began to imagine what it would be like to go on an adventure herself. Then she opened the book and began reading, feeling immediately transported to the harsh deserts of the Old West. The sun shone down, warming her fur, and the smell of sagebrush tickled her nose. Sighing, she wondered what it would be like to actually visit a place like that.

Soon her daydreaming was interrupted by the sound of the door opening. "Daisy May, have you seen enough of the Isle of Manhattan for today?" chirped Mrs. Z. Now seventy years old, Mrs. Z had lived in the apartment for the last thirty years. She always kept a tidy home with everything in its place. All her pictures hanging on the wall were dusted daily and perfectly perpendicular to her pristine white-carpeted floors. Sometimes Daisy May felt as if she and Mrs. Z were like an old married couple living together in the tiny New York City apartment. Their home was nothing like the rugged, adventurous places Daisy May read about in her books, but its predictability and comforts were reassuring.

From her spot on her pillow, Daisy responded groggily, "Yes, I believe I have seen enough. The pizza delivery man turned left just as I predicted he would."

"Well, here's something you didn't predict. You got a package today from Philomena," announced Mrs. Z.

"For me?" asked Daisy, excited since she never received mail. She looked at the package. The address scribbled in the upper left corner read: "22 Lamy Station Trail, Lamy, New Mexico."

Daisy pawed at the tape and, with Mrs. Z's help, opened the package. It contained a photograph of a skinny, freckled, tan young girl standing confidently in bright sunlight. She wore a beat-up, faded canvas sun hat, a khaki safari-type shirt with double chest pockets, cargo shorts with matching pockets on both sides, and tall lace-up leather boots. A rucksack was flung across her shoulder. "Now here's a girl who's seen many adventures," Daisy thought.

"My, she's looking more mature these days. Goodness, how time flies. She must be about nine years old already," said Mrs. Z.

"Looks like she's dressed for adventure. Is she going on an expedition?" asked Daisy.

Mrs. Z smiled and said, "My granddaughter has always loved adventure. But I think she likes to dress like her father, Marco. Remember I told you a while ago that he's a paleontologist? He travels a lot, looking for dinosaur bones. He's on a dig in North Dakota right now."

"Yes. I do remember," replied Daisy, recalling how she had thought Marco had an adventurous job. But Daisy believed she had heard something like disapproval in Mrs. Z's voice, something she was not used to hearing from the usually cheerful and supportive Mrs. Z.

Daisy sniffed the air. An exotic fragrant scent was emanating from the package. Mrs. Z pulled out a few sprigs of a plant Daisy didn't recognize. It smelled smoky and sweet at the same time.

"It's sagebrush," Mrs. Z explained. "It grows all over New Mexico."

"So that's what the West smells like," Daisy said, her mind again drifting to the pages of her latest western novel.

"Oh, look. There's a letter. It's also addressed to you, Daisy," said Mrs. Z.

As Mrs. Z placed the letter in front of her, Daisy leaned closer and read:

Dear Daisy May,

I'm writing to you from Lamy, New Mexico, where I live with my family. I think you know all this, but I wanted to refresh your memory since we have not talked in a long time.

Maybe this sounds weird, but over the last couple of weeks I've had what my mom calls "serial dreams." In these dreams, I'm not alone like I am most of the time. We are walking together, and I'm holding half of some valuable object, like a gift, and you're holding the other half, and the only way we can both have it is if we combine our two halves. My mom says that when someone has powerful dreams like this it's important to pay attention because they guide you to positive things in life.

Some other mysterious things happening here in Lamy are in my dreams. I wish I could say more, but it really feels like we are meant to investigate the things that are happening and do something great together. Our family has known for a long time that you have special powers that other cats could only dream of. So, I'm inviting you out to Lamy. Inside is a train ticket. Please come join me in New Mexico and see if we can discover the meaning of my dreams and solve some mysteries.

—Philomena

Daisy looked up at Mrs. Z and remarked, "How strange. It sounds like a mystery novel."

"This doesn't surprise me. My daughter has always taught Philomena to trust her instincts, think for herself, be curious about things, and use her intuition as a guide to action," commented Mrs. Z.

Noticing something taped to the picture of Philomena, with Mrs. Z's help Daisy turned it over, peeled an envelope from the picture, and opened it. "It's a train ticket to New Mexico," said Daisy tentatively.

"How exciting! You could use a good trip, Daisy," said Mrs. Z.

"New Mexico? Me?" Daisy replied, suddenly feeling apprehensive. "It would be hot and dry, and I wouldn't have my purple pillow, or Mrs. Z to bring me milk in my favorite bowl. But it might be fun to have such an adventure and solve some mysteries," she thought.

"Sounds like you have a choice to make, Daisy," Mrs. Z interrupted. "I know you've fallen into a pretty dull routine here. And I also know that you would jump at the opportunity to use your special psychic powers for something more adventurous and important than predicting the movements of pedestrians on the street from a pillow in a New York apartment building."

"But who would keep you company?" Daisy countered.

"We are all creatures of habit, Daisy, but there are times when the predictable road, the easy road, is not the one to take. You have a golden opportunity to break free for a while and explore a new place with Philomena," Mrs. Z said.

Daisy looked up at Mrs. Z, who knelt down to her, petted her on the head, and added, "I will miss you terribly, but you're going. Philomena needs you, and I think you might need her."

With that, Mrs. Z walked away, leaving Daisy too stunned to move. Daisy's fur tingled, which she recognized as a sign that something important had been said or done that related to a bigger perspective of life.

As night approached and the lights of the city came up, making the raindrops on the passing cars sparkle, Daisy continued to fret about the possibility of traveling to New Mexico. She burrowed into her pillow, trying to calm her nerves in the comfort of its soft cloth. "Perhaps I just need a good night's sleep," she thought. Usually, the hypnotizing sound of falling rain lulled Daisy to sleep, but tonight was different. She kept curling and uncurling her furry body, trying to get comfortable. Eventually, she drifted off to sleep and began to dream.

In her dream, she saw a Native American man standing on a mountaintop at sunset smiling at her. The man was slender, with salt-and-pepper hair pulled back in a tight ponytail, seeming young despite his age. Standing beside the man was a girl who looked like Philomena. Daisy could tell they were close, like a student and a teacher. They both smiled warmly to Daisy and beckoned her to follow them into the surrounding desert. As Daisy began to follow, with a sense of camaraderie, the golden light of the desert sunset changed into a field of brilliant stars. Then the man and girl disappeared, and Daisy was alone. The scene disappeared and was replaced by the image of an old, dark, faded painting. The painting was too dark to view clearly, but its enormity gave Daisy the strangest feeling that it looked more like a doorway than a painting. Then, without being aware of what she was doing, Daisy leapt through it, surprised by the feeling of exhilaration and freedom she experienced.

The next day dawned bright and clear. Daisy was unusually drowsy as she slowly lifted her head from her pillow, trying to shake off the remnants of her dream. She looked out the window to see that the city had a freshly scrubbed look that only happened after a few days of purifying rain. As the early morning sunlight warmed Daisy's fur, she realized that she also felt different somehow, as though her confusion and apprehension had been washed away and she could see more clearly. It was as if she was standing in the middle of a balanced fulcrum: on one side were all the predictable comforts of her home and on the other the tantalizing chance to experience a whole new world of discovery, friendship, and adventure, a world that had already invaded her dreams. She now had an unshakable certainty that a journey to New Mexico, although unknown terrain, would be potentially rewarding.

"Mrs. Z, I had a very unusual dream last night," Daisy declared as Mrs. Z placed her bowl of milk in front of her.

"Were you floating down the Nile being fed peeled grapes, my dear?" quipped Mrs. Z.

"No grapes, but I saw myself following a man and a girl in a place I did not know then taking the biggest leap of faith in my life!" exclaimed Daisy.

"Dreams are powerful things," Mrs. Z said as she walked toward her bedroom closet and pulled out a dusty backpack. "This once belonged to Philomena's mother, Antoinette. I had a feeling it would come in handy some-day. I think it's time we get you ready for your journey."

"Mrs. Z, I'll need my little knit sweater. I hear it gets very cold at night in the desert," Daisy said confidently.

"That's my girl," said Mrs. Z, proudly.

"I can do this, I can do this," thought Daisy. "If I get into scary situations, I'll have Philomena with me. Besides, I am eager for any chance to use my special psychic powers and see if I was indeed meant for great-ness as the woman at the animal shelter said." A feeling of delicious anticipation washed over her, a feeling she could not remember ever having before.

# CHAPTER 2

Philomena had walked by the Pink Garter Saloon countless times before since it was a prominent land-mark in her hometown. But now hanging on its wall was a mystery that drew her to it: a painting that for weeks had seemed to be changing before her very eyes. She thought to herself, "If Daddy can solve million-year-old mysteries by digging up ancient dinosaur bones, I know I can figure out what's going on with this painting."

It was Community Day, and most residents of Lamy, New Mexico, had turned out to celebrate the summer solstice. Philomena made a point of entering the Pink Garter Saloon at the end of the party because she didn't want other people around when she carried out her plan.

After everyone had left the saloon, she pulled her camera out of her backpack and stood in front of the old painting of a Native American man crouching on a rock surrounded by tall prairie grass and teepees. Before taking a shot, she looked around to make sure she was not being watched. For weeks now, she had kept a record of the mysterious subtle changes in the painting. She reflected on when she'd first noticed the immense, dark presence glowering down at her from its perch in the darkest part of the saloon and how something unexplainable about it had fired her imagination. She would stand in front of it for what seemed like hours, thinking to herself, "Maybe this is what great artists do—paint works of art that allow your imagination to soar." In the beginning, it seemed like only the background changed. But she was pretty sure the painting was now changing in more ways.

Philomena aimed her camera at the painting, looking closely at every detail, all magically alive somehow. Suddenly, she heard a floorboard squeak. Quickly, she hid her camera in the left pocket of her cargo pants and whirled around to see a sixteen-year-old boy approaching.

"Grady, don't sneak up on me like that!" Philomena barked.

Grady stepped out of the shadows, pointed a finger at Philomena, and said, "You are so weird, Philly! What are you doing with that painting?"

Philomena cringed at the nickname, patted her camera flat against her cargo pocket, and replied, "None of your business, Grady. And my name is Philomena."

"You're not supposed to be here, Philly. You're up to something. I know it," Grady said, his eyes narrowing.

"Well, it's really none of your business, but if you must know I am an art lover, and I particularly like this painting," Philomena countered. Grady crossed his arms over his chest. "Besides, if I'm not supposed to be here, then what are *you* doing here?" Philomena added, stepping out into the cool New Mexico night.

Philomena realized that she'd have to keep an eye on Grady. She had always thought he was a sad case, depressed and angry as if something was eating at him. But she thought, "At least he doesn't have a father who's never home."

As she walked home, Philomena concluded that she needed to talk to her artist friend Noshi about this strange painting. He always had good advice, and he was like a second father to her, especially when her dad, Marco, was away. And he knew a lot about paintings and the imagination. But first she needed Daisy to come help her investigate this mystery.

After much frustrating gymnastic experimentation, Daisy had finally found a comfortable position in the train car. She leaned against the cold metal wall and used her backpack as a pillow on the seat next to her. She was hungry and sore all over, and she hadn't been able to get a wink of sleep. She was already missing her pillow and bowl of milk and the view of the city from her favorite perch.

The train entered a dark, narrow winding canyon, and Daisy imagined a bunch of desperados hidden there, ready to jump onto the train just like in her novels. She never would have guessed when she was reading those western stories that she'd actually have a chance to experience the Old West. Eventually, she relaxed enough to let the rhythmic hum of the wheels lull her to sleep.

"Arriving in Lamy, New Mexico," boomed a scratchy voice over the loudspeaker.

Daisy sat up, alert in an instant, realizing that she was finally at her destination. Lamy looked like a sleepy little toy town with its squat adobe buildings dotting the hillsides, its tiny train station, and no paved roads. As she gazed out the window, Daisy was surprised by a sudden flood of images and feelings, including a sense that the town she had entered was there but not there, that somehow it could simply go in and out of existence. "What a strange sensation," she thought. "It's as though I've passed over some kind of threshold between reality and fantasy." In that moment, she didn't feel like a cat but like a lone traveler in time and space on a voyage far from her home.

Some other details about the town struck her immediately: there were two single train cars on a set of railroad tracks to the right of the track on which her train was traveling, and one of the cars was hidden behind what appeared to be large cottonwood trees. She remembered from her western novels that cottonwood trees in the Southwest grew close to rivers and turned a beautiful golden color in the fall. Just the faintest glint of silver through those trees betrayed the hidden train. Daisy pressed her face so close to the glass that condensation

began to form on the window, making the little town look even more otherworldly.

Daisy's train passed the train car hidden in the trees and then came up on the other train car. Daisy noticed that this one was different. It had a domed, dull silver top with many windows; the lower half was a rusty red- dish brown; and it looked neglected. "I wonder if it's a working train car or if it's just been left there to rot," she thought. She made a mental note to ask Philomena about the two apparently abandoned train cars.

Daisy's train finally screeched to a halt, and a young boy, who was traveling with his family on the train, helped Daisy put on Philomena's old backpack, which Mrs. Z had modified perfectly to fit her feline physique. The boy patted Daisy on her furry head and asked, "Are you coming home or traveling somewhere?"

Daisy furrowed her brow a little and replied, "I'm not really sure right now. Maybe a little of both."

The door of the train opened, and Daisy hopped down onto the metal footstool placed there, feeling like she'd arrived on another planet. The hot, dry air felt very for- eign to a New York cat accustomed to humidity, and when she looked up she saw a sky bluer than any she had ever seen. The skies back home were usually hazy and appeared mostly as slivers peeking through tower- ing buildings. This New Mexico sky vaulting above her and stretching to the horizon made her so dizzy she almost fell off the stool.

Before she could get her bearings, she heard her name being called as Philomena ran to her. An exhausted Daisy fell into Philomena's waiting arms, feeling all the weariness of her cross-country journey. She fondly recalled the last time Philomena had visited Mrs. Z's apartment and that she had sensed something special about the girl, believing she would do big things in her life.

"I knew you'd come!" said Philomena, beaming at Daisy. "Grandma Z told me you'd be on this train!" Philomena was wearing the exact clothes she wore in the picture she had mailed to Daisy, making her look like a slender tomboy dressed like a safari guide.

"The sky is too big and too blue here. When I breathe in, my nostrils hurt. And even the ground feels different, like I'm walking on hot coals!" Daisy complained.

Gently putting Daisy back on the train station's platform, Philomena stated, "You're breathing some of the thinnest, driest air in the whole country, and the sun is really strong here. We're seven thousand feet closer to it!"

Daisy composed herself and quipped, "You look like you're ready to travel somewhere adventurous."

Philomena struck a pose like a superhero, with her legs far apart and her skinny, freckled arms on her hips, and replied, "You know, everyone here says that about me. I like to wear clothes that make me feel ready!"

"Ready for what?" Daisy asked.

"Anything," Philomena proclaimed.

Daisy saw a girl with more confidence than Daisy herself had ever felt, and yet Philomena's stance also reflected something Daisy couldn't quite understand.

"You must be hungry after such a long journey, right?" asked Philomena.

Daisy nodded.

"The diner, a dining car, is just behind the train station, Daisy, and I know the chef. Come on." Philomena began marching toward the train station at a brisk pace, with Daisy hurrying to catch up with her. As they got closer, Daisy noticed that the diner sat on the same abandoned track as the two train cars she'd observed coming into the station. And hitched to a railing near the dining car she saw bicycles, motorcycles, and even a horse.

As if anticipating Daisy's next question, Philomena said, "It used to be a working track, but now only a couple cars sit on it."

Daisy thought she saw Philomena bite down on her lower lip when she mentioned the cars, and sensed that they might be part of the mystery Philomena had encountered.

A wooden stairway was the only entrance to the dining car, and there was a wide gap between each step.

"Do you need help climbing the stairs, Daisy?" asked Philomena.

"I think I can hop it," Daisy replied. Philomena opened a heavy metal door, Daisy entered, and they walked down a narrow corridor to the diner. Immediately, all five of her senses were assaulted. The smell was unlike any Daisy had ever experienced. "What is that smell? It's kind of spicy and sweet."

Philomena laughed and replied, "That's green chile. It's kinda like our state's official spicy vegetable. We put it in lots of things—eggs, soup, stews, bread, and even chocolate!"

The dark corridor opened to a bright, buzzing dining car, echoing with the clanking of silverware. As they walked the narrow aisle between tables, it seemed that everyone in the diner knew Philomena. Daisy noted all the different types of people and styles of clothes they were wearing. There were couples in leather motorcycle jackets, weathered cowboys in dusty blue denim jeans, families, teenagers and infants, and a very fit older couple wearing colorful spandex bicycle shorts and neon green-and-yellow cycling tops.

"There's an empty table," Philomena said, pointing to the back of the diner. As they walked down the aisle, a boy stuck his leg out and blocked their way, which Daisy considered rude.

"Hey, art lover, who's your friend?" said the boy.

Philomena whispered to Daisy, "That's Grady. He's bad news. Just ignore him. He's never happy wherever he is and makes everyone else unhappy." Philomena looked up at Grady with a steely stare and demanded, "Grady, move your leg and let us pass . . . or else."

Daisy was aghast; she had never heard anybody talk like that before. Mrs. Z always spoke in a gentle, soothing, cultured voice.

Grady smirked and then slowly retracted his leg and let them pass. As Daisy padded by the boy, she snuck a glance at him. He was slender like Philomena and wore beat-up dark jeans and a black T-shirt that read "They Live" in worn, stenciled letters. Daisy looked back as they passed the boy and saw him put his index and middle fingers up to his eyes, as if to say, "I'm watching you."

As Philomena slid into their booth at the back of the diner, she remarked, "Grady is like my arch nemesis. I was doing research in the saloon across the street, and he snuck up on me." Philomena directed Daisy to look out the train car window in the direction of an old-looking saloon.

Daisy thought it looked like the perfect location for a movie about the Old West, but she also sensed something mysterious behind those doors, and her fur tingled. "Research?" she inquired.

Before Philomena could answer, a wild-looking, heavy-set man with unruly brown curls and wearing an apron splashed with brown, red, yellow, and green came bounding up the narrow aisle toward them. "Mena! You should have called ahead. I would have reserved a table for you and your friend," the man boomed.

"Michael, this is my friend Daisy. She's from New York City. I just picked her up at the station," Philomena replied.

Michael thrust a big, sweaty hand in Daisy's direction. Daisy straightened up and placed her dainty paw in his enormous mitt and said, "Pleasure to meet you, Michael."

The big man replied, "Oh, you're one of the special cats. We don't get too many talking cats around here, so I'm always honored to meet one."

"Michael owns this diner," Philomena explained. "He makes the best green chile cheeseburgers in the world."

Michael let out a big laugh. "Well, Mena, folks around here do love them, but I think you're engaging in a little culinary hyperbole when you call my burgers the best in the world!" He looked down at Daisy and asked, "You must be famished after such a long trip. What do you fancy, Daisy?"

Philomena leaned in close to Daisy and whispered, "Get the specialty of the house. You won't be disappointed. Don't worry, Daisy, I'll help you eat it."

Daisy didn't want to offend Michael and his world-famous green chile cheeseburger, even if she had no idea what it was. "A green chile cheeseburger, please. But can you make it with a little less green chile, Michael?" she asked.

"You betcha! Iced teas?" Michael asked.

"Yes, please," Philomena replied.

Michael walked off to start their order, and Daisy settled into the leather booth, glad to no longer be in motion. Philomena helped her place her backpack on the leather seat next to her then scanned the diner like a desperado. Daisy was about to inquire after Philomena's behavior when Philomena leaned in close and said, "I want to give you a map I drew up." Philomena pulled out a piece of folded white notebook paper from her backpack and slid it across the table to Daisy. "If we ever get separated, you'll need this. It'll help you find your way."

Daisy's fur tingled again as she looked at the map. At the upper right corner was a house on top of a mountain. Philomena had also drawn the abandoned railroad track

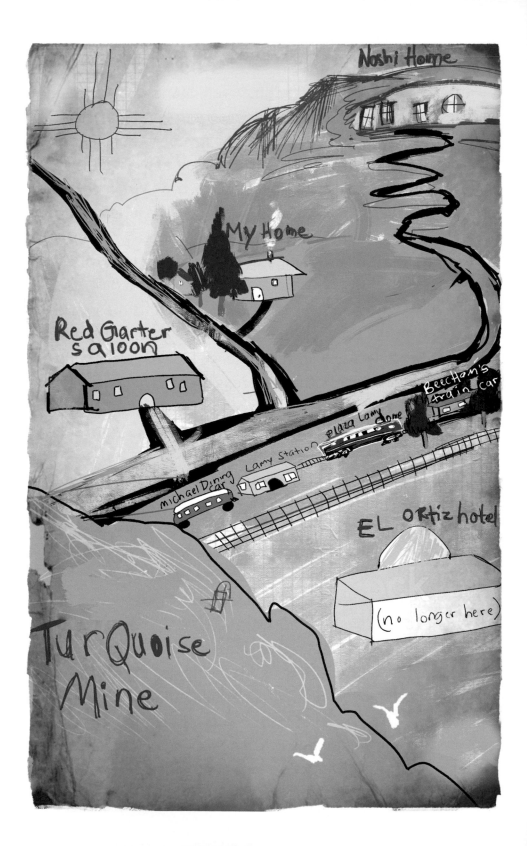

with the two railroad cars Daisy had seen from the train window. "Lamy must be a bizarre place," she thought.

"That's Noshi's home," Philomena explained, pointing to the house. "He's my friend and an artist, and sort of a second dad to me, especially when my dad is traveling. We need to visit him soon. I have important questions to ask him." As Daisy pondered Philomena's cryptic words, she saw Michael bounding toward their table with two plates piled high with steaming food.

"Here ya go. Two of my green chile cheeseburgers. One hot and one not...for the novice!" said Michael, winking at Daisy before returning to the kitchen. Daisy looked wide-eyed at the biggest burger she had ever seen.

Philomena let out a deep belly laugh and said, kindly, "Eat only as much as you want. You can save the rest for later."

Daisy wasn't sure how to begin eating the giant burger. Finally, she opened her small mouth as wide as she could and, with Philomena holding the burger steady, gamely chomped down on it. Warm, gooey cheese and spicy green chile filled her mouth and ran down her chin. There was only one word to describe it: *delicious*.

"I take it you approve," Philomena said.

"Oh. It's the best thing I've ever eaten," Daisy replied, her mouth still half full of burger. In New York, Mrs. Z had occasionally treated her to hot dogs when they went to parks, but green chile cheeseburgers were even more wonderful.

Daisy and Philomena ate in silence for several minutes. At last, Daisy sat back, unable to eat another bite. Philomena had nearly finished, as well.

Daisy figured it was time to start understanding why Philomena had sent for her. "Your letter was very mysterious. I got the sense you weren't telling me everything. After I read your letter, I had a very power-ful dream about you and another person—an older man, maybe a friend or teacher. And then I found myself in front of an enormous painting. But it was also a door-way, and I leapt through it," Daisy said.

Philomena looked up, her eyes wide. Daisy continued in a hushed voice, knowing she had hit on something big, "And just as my train was pulling in to Lamy today I had the strangest feeling that I was entering an illu-sion, a Swiss-cheese reality where things can suddenly change and time can move forward and backward in mysterious ways. Does any of this make sense to you or is my imagination running away with me?"

Philomena scanned the diner to make sure no one was listening then leaned in close to Daisy's furry ear and whispered, "I don't know how you know these things, but they are all true. I was in the saloon across the street, and there's a painting on the wall in there that's changing. I've proved this by taking photos of it over time. I'm not sure why this is happening. Maybe imagination is somehow involved. I have a special gift of a vivid imagination like your psychic sense."

Just then, a girl at least two years younger than Phi-lomena came racing up the diner's narrow aisle looking upset and shaky. Philomena immediately stood up and held the girl in her arms.

"MacCaully, what's wrong?" Philomena asked.

It seemed to Daisy that Philomena was sort of like the sun, with others in Lamy like planets revolving around her. She had an inner strength, charisma, and gusto for life that others were apparently drawn to—like this girl.

"Grady did it again. He mistreated Rama," MacCaully said in a distraught voice.

Daisy watched as Philomena glowered at Grady, who was still sitting a few booths away from them. Philomena put her arm around MacCaully's shoulder. Slowly, Mac-Caully pulled herself together. Daisy felt bad for her; she seemed so young and vulnerable compared to Philomena.

"Okay. Just take a deep breath and tell me what happened," Philomena said.

"Rama tore up his neck and chest trying to push down his barbed-wire pen because Grady forgot to feed him again," replied MacCaully.

"Does Rama need medical attention?" asked Philomena.

MacCaully said, "No, he'll be okay. The scratches aren't bad."

Philomena's eyes got a steely look about them, and she said, "I'm going to give that boy a talking to. He can't go around abusing animals, particularly Rama . . . he's special."

Daisy turned and saw Grady walking out of the diner. She wondered what would make a boy so mean-spirited.

Philomena asked MacCaully, "What about your folks?"

"They're too busy with the business in Santa Fe, so they put Grady in charge of taking care of my llama. But he always forgets to feed him, and I'm too small to carry the hay bales. And now Rama's injured." Philomena guided MacCaully into the booth and then sat down beside her.

"My brother is such a jerk," MacCaully said, stuffing one of Philomena's fries in her mouth.

Daisy looked at Philomena for a reaction and saw her stifle a chuckle.

"Don't worry, we'll figure something out. Mac, this is my friend Daisy from New York City. I asked her to come stay with me for a while," said Philomena.

"Pleased to meet you," said Daisy.

MacCaully shook Daisy's paw and said in a small voice, "New York City! I've never been someplace so big. Rama sometimes talks to us, too, but almost never to Grady because he says it's like talking to a wall. What's New York City like?"

"It's an amazing place. Full of all types of people and crazy tall buildings. And you can get anything you want at any hour of the day or night," Daisy explained.

"Wow!" exclaimed MacCaully.

Daisy chuckled to herself. It had been a long time since she'd thought of New York with that kind of awe. She stared into MacCaully's big eyes and for a moment was impressed that MacCaully, a girl younger than Philomena, didn't flinch when she started talking to her, which told her that MacCaully was a special soul who would seek out experiences that would widen her world beyond Lamy. Suddenly, she surprised herself by saying, "MacCaully, something tells me that extraordinary experiences await you and your llama. You both are special. Stay close to him. He needs you, and you need him."

With these words, Daisy's fur tingled and she felt content that she had used her powers of perception to be of service to MacCaully for a good cause. It was like the feeling she got when she played her game of precognitive people-watching in her window back home, but instead of knowing the direction in which people would turn down the street she had suddenly known what direction Mac-Caully would take in life. The feeling was a little strange for her, but she knew she'd become more familiar with it in time. Daisy looked up to see Philomena staring at her, a knowing smile rising at the corners of her mouth. Daisy wondered what that meant.

"Daisy just arrived, and I want to show her around town. If Grady does any more boneheaded things, call my mom. She'll give your brother a piece of her mind!" declared Philomena.

MacCaully gave Philomena a big hug, patted Daisy on her head, and said, "Nice to meet you, Daisy. I hope I see you again before you leave."

"I would like that very much," Daisy responded.

After MacCaully walked out the diner door, Philomena rummaged in her backpack then said, "First, look at these pictures I took in the Pink Garter Saloon." Philomena pulled out five photographs of the painting. Daisy leaned closer to investigate the images.

"I know they're all shot in dim light, but look at the teepees in the background of the first photo, behind that rock formation," continued Philomena.

Daisy looked closer and saw what seemed like a muscular, bare-chested Native American man crouching on

top of a craggy rock in the fading light of a sunset partially eclipsed by ominous storm clouds. He appeared to
be looking into the distance at something he was wary
of. Daisy had the sense that he did not want to be seen
by what he was looking at. She said, "Do you mean
here, off in the right corner—the little white teepees?"

"Yes," Philomena said, leaning further forward.

Daisy's eyes widened as she looked from the first
photo to the last, noticing that there were fewer teepees
in the last photo and that the tall grasses in front of the
teepees seemed subtly different, as though swaying in
the wind, with each photo capturing a slightly different
movement. It was as if the painting was alive. Daisy's
fur tingled again.

"Amazing. It's like the painting changed. But how
could that be? How far apart in time were the photos
taken?" Daisy asked.

Philomena looked around warily and whispered, "The
last photo was taken a week after the first. I'm sure
other people wander into that dark corner and look at
the painting also...Why don't they see it change?"

Daisy responded, thoughtfully, "I think we all have
special powers we might not know about. Your special
power seems to be your imagination, making things
come alive."

Daisy ran her paws gently over all five photos. Again
her fur tingled, and she said, "This painting looks like the
image from my dream, the one I had before I came here."

Philomena said, gazing intently, "We have to get into
the Pink Garter Saloon when it's not open so we can look

at the painting without anyone getting suspicious. Grady already caught me once. I wonder if we should see Noshi first. I have a feeling he might have some answers for us." With that, Philomena put the photos back in her pack then added, "Daisy, it's time we get this adventure started."

Daisy looked down at her enormous half-eaten cheeseburger and confessed, "I've never eaten this much food in one sitting in all my life. I don't think I can manage another bite."

"That's okay. We can pack it up and take it with us," Philomena replied.

As they left the diner, Daisy had a realization—that during this visit to Lamy, New Mexico, she would need to use her powers of perception and clairvoyance to a greater extent than ever before and that her experiences would change her forever. As she thought of this, her fur tingled. She knew with certainty that she was growing in this new world full of mysteries.

# CHAPTER 3

As Daisy and Philomena stepped out into the bright Lamy sun, a big dusty pickup truck came barreling down the dirt road toward them, honking. Just before Daisy could panic, Philomena scooped her up in her arms protectively. As the pickup truck passed them, Daisy could see that an old man was sitting in the bed clutching a tiny black puppy that was partially hidden inside his white shirt. Upon seeing Daisy and Philomena, the man seemed to come out of a stupor and shouted, "Did you see the stars all fall down last night?"

Daisy thought he might be drunk or crazy. As the truck picked up speed, he waved his arms wildly upward to the sky and shouted, "I saw it, I saw it!"

Philomena looked very annoyed.

"Who was that?" Daisy asked.

"I don't know, and I'm sorry he came by when he did," Philomena said, still holding Daisy. "Come on. My house is just up this way. Maybe my mom is still home." Philomena leaned close to her new friend and whispered conspiratorially, "I haven't told Mom about the painting yet. Let's keep that a secret for now, okay?" Daisy nodded but wondered silently why Philomena would keep any secrets from her mother.

Philomena placed Daisy on the warm ground, and they walked up the road together. As they approached Philomena's home, Daisy noticed an enormous Ponderosa pine tree almost blocking her view of the house. Daisy craned her neck skyward to take in the whole tree. When she was a kitten, Mrs. Z had taken her to Rockefeller Center once to see the famous Christmas tree, and she'd never forgotten how impressive it had looked all decked out in festive ornaments. Daisy thought Philomena's tree was at least as tall. Suddenly, she heard a muffled flutter of wings coming from the top of the tree.

"Oh, that's Bishop Lamy and his wife, Willa. Mom named them after two famous people who lived in New Mexico many years ago," Philomena said. "They've lived in our big tree for years, and sometimes they even follow me when I go on adventures."

Just then two gray doves swooped out of the tree and hovered above them. For a moment, Daisy was startled but managed to say, "Hello, Bishop and Willa." They seemed to bob their heads in response, unfazed by communicating with a cat.

As Daisy and Philomena entered the house, Daisy was in awe of it. She was only familiar with tiny match-box apartments stacked one upon another until they reached high in the sky above Manhattan. But this was a real home. She immediately noticed the high vaulted ceiling and was reminded of a photo she had seen in one of Mrs. Z's fancy European magazines of a beautiful, rustic country house.

"Hi, Mom, we're home," Philomena said in a sing-song voice as she casually threw her backpack onto the kitchen table, removed her sun hat, and shook her unruly hair. When no one answered, Philomena walked to a side table and explained, "She always leaves me a little note when she goes out."

Daisy was a little embarrassed to ask the question she had in mind but decided to anyway. "Your mom trusts you to be home all alone?" Daisy could sense that Philomena was a little defensive about her question, so she quickly added, "You must be a very independent and mature girl for your mother to trust you so much."

Philomena sighed and replied, "They both know I'm sort of independent. I like being alone mostly, except when I don't." Philomena looked at her friend and confided, "My daddy loves his work. He told me that digging for dinosaurs is like being a time traveler who can look back millions and millions of years into the earth's past. He often says, 'I know you understand, Philomena. You and I are from the same tribe of adventurers. We constantly seek and discover new things, which brings us great joy. It's our reason for living, I think.'" Philomena's face lost some of its glow as she reflected on her father. She loved the freedom she had, but the darker side of the equation was that she felt isolated and lonely much of the time.

Hiding under a glass cover that looked like a big hat were foil-wrapped sandwiches, home-baked cookies, a note, and a letter. Philomena read the note:

Sorry, sweetheart, I had to run some errands in Santa Fe and will miss our Daisy's arrival, but I made you guys sandwiches and a batch of yummy cookies. Please eat the sandwiches first! I got a phone call from your father. He was so sorry to have missed you. He's excited that he discovered an almost fully intact triceratops about 65 million years old! He said he'll be delayed in coming home, maybe staying a month more in North Dakota. He said there's been an unexpected development, and he needs to process a treasure trove of information. He wrote you a letter. I'll be back in a couple of hours.

Love,
Mom

P.S. Welcome to Lamy, Daisy!

Daisy could tell Philomena was upset and said, consolingly, "You must be disappointed. I'm sorry you have to wait so long before your father returns."

Philomena patted Daisy on her head and replied defiantly, "That's okay. We have each other now, and we have our adventures to come. I just wish I could have more adventures with him, too." As strong as Philomena appeared to be, it was clear to Daisy that she had a deep wound of loneliness because of her father's frequent absences even though she tried to mask it. Daisy resolved to stay supportive of Philomena.

Philomena crumpled up the note, lifted the glass jar, and took out two large chocolate chip cookies for her and Daisy. As Philomena ate one of the cookies, she explained, "Mom says I'm a lot like my daddy Marco. He likes being alone in nature. She says I'm a funny bunny because I only want to go my way and nobody else's. You know, Daisy, I think I'm actually really lucky that I have two parents who like adventure. My mom once lived in New York City and was a professional actress! That sounds super exciting, doesn't it?"

Daisy nodded enthusiastically, nibbled her cookie, and said, "Just think where your father is now—digging for dinosaurs in North Dakota. That's really adventurous."

Philomena nodded, then grew thoughtful and confessed, "And I am also adventurous, different from other kids around here. I don't really hang out with any of them, except for MacCaully sometimes, but she's kinda young. I'd rather walk the train tracks alone, dig up old stuff, and go on hikes in the mountains. When Mom realized I was so much like Dad, she decided to help me be more adventurous, too. She knew I was going to need something to carry all my important stuff in when I went on solo adventures, so she found this leather backpack in an old thrift store in Santa Fe. When she gave it to me, she said, 'This looks like a Philomena backpack.'"

Daisy finished the cookie and asked, "What kinds of things do you put in the backpack?"

"Every adventure is a little different and requires different tools. For instance, tonight we'll need pliers, a wool bedroll, two pillows, a flashlight, our yummy leftovers from dinner, and maybe a few more items," Philomena explained.

Daisy asked, "Aren't we sleeping in your home tonight?"

"Not tonight, Daisy. I'm taking you to a special, top-secret place not far from here. You're going to love it! What's really special about the high desert of New Mexico is the great outdoors," Philomena stated confidently. "We have plans to make and mysteries to solve."

Although Daisy was a little disappointed that after her long cross-country journey she was not going to be able to sleep in a comfortable bed that night, she nevertheless was excited about the possibility of seeing the secret place and solving some mysteries.

As the afternoon wore on, Daisy began experiencing mixed emotions about her whirlwind introduction to Philomena's dramatic world. On the one hand, she enjoyed Philomena's company as she was energetic, entertaining, charismatic, confident, and adventurous. On the other hand, Daisy found it unsettling that Philomena's mother left her alone and that her father was away for extended periods of time. Mrs. Z was never very far away for long. In fact, she almost hovered over Daisy most of the time.

But this was a different kind of family with an only child who showed an independence and strength beyond her years. Still, it was clear that Philomena felt sadness about her father and missed him terribly. Daisy thought, "What a curious portrait of a young girl she is—fearless and confident. Yet maybe she masks her loneliness by engaging in adventures and solving mysteries." Daisy recalled a kindly old Chinese neighbor of Mrs. Z's who had a saying that Daisy thought rang true: "The bigger the front, the bigger the back." Daisy understood this to mean that the face we show the world, whether it is one of confidence, strength, fear, or humor, is usually hiding the true self, which could be the exact opposite. She wondered to what degree this old saying was true for Philomena.

They were in Philomena's room preparing for their overnight adventure when the front door opened and Philomena's mother, Antoinette, shouted cheerfully, "Hi, sweetheart. I'm home! Do we have a distinguished visitor from New York with us?" No sooner had Philomena picked up Daisy and taken her to the front room than a very fashionable, tall, and slender woman wafted in wearing a crisp white shirt with an upturned collar, blue jeans in a perfect shade of blue that seemed to match her eyes, and lots of jewelry. Daisy immediately felt as though she were in the presence of a movie star. Mrs. Z, from time to time, had shared pictures of her daughter, but being in her presence was almost breathtaking. Daisy immediately noted that Philomena's mother did not look like most of the people who'd been eating lunch in Michael's dining car. Even though she was dressed rather casually, there was an air of elegance about her.

"I've missed you so much, Daisy," Antoinette said, nuzzling her.

As Antoinette came close to her, Daisy got a good look at her jewelry, including about ten different bracelets on her left arm. "I recognize some of your bracelets from the photos Mrs. Z showed me, but you seem to have added more," Daisy remarked.

Antoinette started to finger each bracelet as though there were an entire cherished story behind its purchase. "Over the last twenty years of travel, I've managed to collect more and more of them. This one is from South Africa; this one from Guatemala; and so forth."

Daisy thought Antoinette was very different from Mrs. Z, even though she was her daughter. She was an original. In fact, she and her daughter Philomena were both originals—unique people who were not afraid to express their personalities.

"What are your plans, ladies?" asked Antoinette as she kissed her daughter.

"I'm taking Daisy to see the Train of Stars tonight. It'll be a perfect night for it. We have much to talk about," Philomena said with great gravity in her voice.

"Do you have all you need, sweetie? Might be a little chilly in there," cautioned Antoinette.

"We'll be fine, Mom," Philomena replied, reassuringly.

Antoinette looked at Daisy and said, "My daughter keeps dropping hints of strange goings on here in our village. Given your powers of perception, I'll bet you can help her solve these mysteries. When I was a young actor in New York City long before Philomena came along, I was in a play about a mystery that only got solved in the very last scene. I still remember how exciting it was to solve the mystery every night." Antoinette looked at her daughter and said playfully, "I wonder if you got your love of mysteries from me instead of your dad?" Daisy could see how Philomena might have gotten her love of mysteries from either of her parents, but she still wondered if some of Philomena's activities stemmed from loneliness.

As the light began fading from the sky, with great deliberateness Philomena placed each item on her list carefully in her backpack, the two large, soft pillows requiring extra effort to squeeze in. Then abruptly, she said, "Daisy, I almost forgot my journal. I do some of my best writing in the Train of Stars." She ran back to her room to get it.

"Time to go," Philomena commanded as she cinched up her shoulder straps tightly.

"Will you two be having breakfast at Michael's diner tomorrow morning or here with me?" Antoinette inquired.

"I think we'll go back to Michael's. Sometimes he makes me a special omelet that I'd like to share with Daisy. Besides, I'm going to take Daisy up to see Noshi first thing, and we'll want a big breakfast to fuel us up," said Philomena.

Smiling, Daisy asked Philomena to grab her scarf and sweater, and they walked out into the crisp evening air. Daisy noticed the doves hovering over their heads and deduced that they watched over Philomena during her many adventures.

"Daisy, stay close to me and watch wherever I beam my flashlight," Philomena advised. Daisy was surprised that the ground had become so much colder than it was when she'd gotten off the train.

Philomena walked across the dirt road and made a left at the train station. The light from the flashlight danced on the ground, illuminating circles of dirt and rock and what looked like old abandoned train tracks. Suddenly, a train car loomed in front of them. Philomena looked around suspiciously and then slipped her backpack off. Daisy noticed some writing on the front of the train that said "Plaza Lamy Dome Car." Then she realized that this was the car she'd spotted from the window of her train just this morning.

"Follow me," Philomena whispered. "I'm going to pry back this section of metal on the back corner of the car with my pliers."

Daisy looked around apprehensively. She could see that the section of metal already had a big crease in it where Philomena had probably worked the metal back from the train car many times. "Have you ever been caught doing this?" Daisy asked.

"Not yet. Not even Grady knows about this," she whispered. Philomena picked up Daisy and carefully pushed her through the opening, mindful to avoid the bent metal.

As Daisy's eyes acclimated to the inky black interior of the train car, she saw her friend slither into the car behind her. "You must have done this many times, Philomena," Daisy said.

Philomena smiled, picked up her flashlight, and aimed it straight into the dark corridor of the train. Daisy began to shake.

"What's wrong, Daisy?" asked Philomena.

"I've never broken into a train before, and I'm quite sure it's illegal!" Daisy said, concerned.

Philomena pointed the flashlight so it beamed light further into the train car and replied reassuringly, "Don't worry, Daisy. I really have done this many times before."

As Daisy felt more reassured, she confessed, "You have to remember something. I was raised as a house cat, even though I'm strong and tough. All these things are new to me." Philomena picked up Daisy protectively, held her close to her chest, and stepped into the train car, illuminated only by the little circle of light from her flashlight.

"Don't worry, I'm going to show you something that will amaze you!" Philomena said. She took Daisy up a narrow spiral staircase where it was much brighter so they could see without the aid of the flashlight. Daisy looked straight up and nearly fainted. There, on the upper deck of the train car, millions of stars were shining down on them through the overhead glass dome.

"I have never seen so many stars in my entire life!" she blurted out, excitedly. Daisy had seen stars back home in New York City, but there were only a handful visible from her apartment, and their light was much fainter than these. There the stars always played hide and seek between the tall buildings that often blocked them from view. As Daisy craned her neck to take in the entire firmament, she gasped, "This is unbelievable!"

"It's my favorite secret place, Daisy," Philomena confided in a hushed voice as she took off her backpack and began pulling out the contents.

"I remember a wonderful trip to the Hayden Planetarium in New York when I was just a kitten. Mrs. Z snuck me in, hidden in her purse, because she wanted me to see important things that other cats did not have the opportunity to experience, such as what the night sky looks like when you travel away from big cities. Sometimes I think that's why I was able to develop my special powers. But this...this is unbelievably beautiful!" Daisy proclaimed.

Daisy was still spellbound, looking at all the brilliant stars set in the darkest sky she'd ever seen, when Philomena said, "It gets quite chilly in the desert at night, but this bedroll is big enough for both of us to sleep on."

After a time, Daisy looked away from the stars and asked Philomena, "Don't you ever get lonely?"

Philomena unraveled the bedroll and patted it smooth as she replied, "I have the things that are most important to me. My mom, my dad when he's home, adventures, and my new friend!" Daisy noted a hint of regret in Philomena's voice but chose not to pursue it further.

Philomena placed the pillows in the center of the bedroll and then reached into her backpack to get the leftovers from the diner. They sat in silence as they ate their dinner under a celestial canopy. They were both aware that their lives had become connected in deep

and mysterious ways. Daisy looked at her friend and thought, "Such a contradiction she is—part young, freckly girl on the verge of becoming a young woman and part independent, mature adventure guide. This adolescent girl represents all the characteristics that I wish I had more of: fearlessness, strength, and that center-of-the-universe feeling she exudes naturally. My strengths may be my powers of intuition, wisdom, and empathy. Maybe the two of us are separate halves of a person puzzle and together we can become whole."

Finally, they surrendered to peaceful slumber. Meanwhile, unbeknownst to Philomena and Daisy, from an infinitely high, distant place, members of the Council of Four gazed down and decided that the two tiny beings would require careful surveillance. One council member said, "There is something quite unusual about these two. We must remain observant. I predict trouble ahead for us."

# CHAPTER 4

*P*op! Pop! Pop! Daisy awoke from a restless sleep alarmed to hear what she thought were gunshots coming from below. She glanced out the window of the train car and saw a grizzled cowboy with a sinister handlebar moustache on a beautiful speckled horse waving two six-shooters in his hands and randomly firing at the sky. Daisy frantically shook Philomena awake.

Philomena growled like a baby bear. Without even looking up to see the source of all the commotion, she comforted Daisy and said matter-of-factly, "Oh, I forgot to tell you about Wyler the cowboy. Every Saturday morning he and his horse, Locomotion, pretend to shoot up the village of Lamy."

"Why would he do that?" asked Daisy.

Philomena rose and joined Daisy at the window to watch Wyler.

"Loco, where the hell is everybody? I'm gonna run outta bullets before anyone sees us," Wyler yelled.

Philomena laughed and then whispered, "He's always wanted to be in the movies. I think he's hoping he'll get noticed by a film producer and cast as a real cowboy."

Daisy replied, "Doesn't he know that only happens in the movies and not in real life?"

Wyler was turning Locomotion in circles in front of the Pink Garter Saloon, appearing to enjoy himself thoroughly. Eventually, he ran out of bullets and stopped spinning.

Philomena said to Daisy, "This is usually when he rides back out of town. He's really harmless and quite sweet."

Daisy had never been awakened by gunfire, even in New York City. She was alarmed to think that a crazy man on horseback simultaneously firing two six-shooters would be considered quite sweet.

Philomena began to roll up the bedroll. "Hungry?" she asked Daisy.

"Sure," Daisy replied in a distracted voice, still in shock over the way she had been awakened.

As they exited the train unnoticed and made their way back to Michael's dining car, Daisy spotted a horse hitched to a wooden post on the west side of the diner. "Is that Wyler's horse?" she asked.

Philomena smirked and replied, "I guess he got tired of trying to be famous...at least for this morning."

Golden fingers of early morning light were reaching into the dining car when Philomena and Daisy entered. As Daisy padded by the other tables, she had the feeling that everyone was looking at her, and wondered how many of the people eating there knew about talking cats. She decided to not talk until she reached her seat, and then only quietly. Daisy had not previously noticed that the walls of the diner were corrugated aluminum and the sun's rays created beautiful reflections that bounced around them in a kaleidoscopic fashion. She had the strangest feeling that the dining car was like a spaceship protecting them against meteors and cosmic radiation from the outer world.

"Philly!" shouted Wyler, whose long, lean legs were stretched out across the narrow aisle. Daisy thought that he must have jumped out of the pages of a western novel.

Philomena tried to make a disapproving face but was not very successful.

"You early birds gotta join me for breakfast. Hey, who's your partner?" Wyler bellowed.

"For just once, Wyler, can you call me by my real name, please?" Philomena pleaded.

Wyler nodded, folded his angular frame back under the table, and motioned for them to join him. "You got a sidekick now?" he inquired.

Philomena proudly responded, "This is my friend Daisy, from the Isle of Manhattan."

Michael bounded down the aisle and said, "I am truly blessed to have you all here this morning. How about some Texas toast, eggs, and hash browns all around?"

Wyler leaned back against the glass window behind him, intertwined his fingers behind his head, and replied, "Suits me just fine, Mr. Michael. Oh, and keep the java flowing, please."

"One of your special omelets to split for Daisy and me," Philomena said.

"Coming right up," Michael replied as he walked off.

Turning back to Philomena, Wyler said, "By the way, I ran into Noshi yesterday, and he told me to tell you that he wants to see you about something. Wouldn't say what, though."

Philomena tried to hide a questioning look on her face and said to Daisy, "I guess we'll hike the mountain this morning and visit Noshi."

"Hey, have either one of you seen that Hollywood producer and his location scout floating around?" asked Wyler. "Loco and me have been working on our galloping and shooting technique."

Philomena replied, "Haven't seen that guy lately. Heard he was scouting up in Abiquiú for a new western called—"

Wyler jumped in to complete Philomena's sentence. "*The Reluctant Cowboy!*"

Soon Michael came lumbering down the aisle, wiping beads of sweat off his forehead and saying, "Hot off the griddle!" Daisy saw what looked like two thick books stacked on a plate, but as Michael got closer to their table she could see that it was two massive slices of toast along with a huge omelet.

Philomena leaned into Daisy and said, "This will be our big meal for the day, Daisy. We'll need all this fuel for the hike up Noshi's mountain."

As he began to devour his Texas toast, Wyler took a long look at Daisy then said, "Daisy, I'm assuming by the way Philomena is communicating with you that you are not from the cat tribe that just plays with yarn absent-mindedly all day but instead belong to the deep-thinking, soulful tribe of talking cats. Am I right?"

Daisy's mouth was too full of toast for her to respond.

"I can answer that!" Philomena jumped in. Philomena looked at her feline friend and proudly declared, "She's of the warrior, adventurer, traveler cat tribe."

Daisy could feel herself blushing under her fur and replied, "Lamy, New Mexico, must be home to the craziest, most original characters in the whole country."

After Wyler had downed four cups of hot coffee and breakfast, he leaned back, patted his now very full stomach, and asked Philomena, "Hey, did you happen to hear about some crazy old coot in the village who was ranting and raving about stars falling out of the sky?"

Daisy immediately recalled the incident with the old pickup truck that had nearly run them over the day before, and her fur began to tingle. She glanced across the road at the Pink Garter Saloon and had the feeling that yesterday's incident was somehow connected to the saloon and maybe to the painting there as well.

"He nearly ran us over yesterday. I'd never seen that guy before," answered Philomena.

"Just another Lamy character, I guess. We got a lot of them," Wyler opined.

Philomena reached into a side pocket of her leather backpack and pulled out a crisp, folded ten-dollar bill. She then took her paper napkin and drew a little picture of the sun hovering in space, looking down over the curve of the earth, and underneath the drawing wrote, "Thank you, Michael. You make the best food in the universe."

As the three of them got up to leave, Philomena said to Daisy, "We'll need to get going soon. It's a long journey up to Noshi's home."

Outside, Wyler unhitched Loco from the post, then said, "Daisy, my cowboy instinct tells me that you and Philomena belong together here in our little village. If I happen to see any movie producers or directors floating around, I'll make sure to tell them that you guys would be great in a young girl/cat buddy movie." With that, Wyler hopped up on Loco and took off.

Philomena remarked, "Strange, Wyler doesn't usually talk so much. He must like you, Daisy."

As they made their way across the road, Philomena pointed to a mountain and said, "We'll need to walk the old dirt road that runs next to the train tracks then climb that mountain to Noshi's house." She added, in response to Daisy's skeptical look, "Don't worry. I have all the supplies we need for our journey right in here." She patted the backpack and struck off into the bright morning sun with Daisy hurrying after her.

It was now late morning, and the desert sun was directly overhead with not a cloud in the sky for even temporary shade. Philomena led, but Daisy could tell she was going at a much slower pace than she would be if traveling alone. As they left town, they made a left turn and followed a dirt road, running parallel to the train tracks, that led into a canyon. Daisy realized that if her paws didn't stay too long on the ground they wouldn't heat up too much, so she adopted a kind of hippity-hop movement that made her seem like a youthful cat. On their right appeared the old train car partially obscured by the three immense cottonwood trees that Daisy had seen when first approaching Lamy. Daisy's fur tingled as she asked, "Does someone live in there?"

"Yeah," said Philomena. "His name is Beecham the Train Man. He lives in that old eighty-foot Hamilton Pullman car most of the year. I've known him all my life, and he's loved trains all his long life. I used to climb the biggest cottonwood tree that leans on the top of his Hamilton."

Daisy couldn't shake the feeling that something was very strange about the train car.

"What's the matter, Daisy? You look like you saw a ghost!" exclaimed Philomena.

Daisy again had the feeling she had on the train as it had slowly pulled into the Lamy station the day before and replied, "I really don't have words to explain it, but it's like time is wonky here and this Pullman car is at the center of it. I get the sensation that this Pullman car is not what it appears to be. Have you ever been inside it?"

Philomena looked quizzically at her friend and answered, "Beecham's invited me to have tea with him from time to time, but I never go past his tiny kitchen. It's very messy in there, and it smells musty."

Daisy sniffed the air and said, "For some reason I get the strangest feeling that there are secrets in there and they involve time and space. There's a busy train station in New York City called Grand Central Station, which is like the hub of a giant wheel with spokes traveling out from the center. Beecham's Pullman car is like that, but it also seems like time flows in more than one direction there. The secrets of Beecham's Pullman car may lie past his kitchen. In fact, there seem to be secrets and strange time anomalies everywhere in Lamy."

Philomena thought a moment and then replied, "You are a very unique cat, Daisy." Philomena then cupped her hands around her mouth and shouted, "Beecham, you in there? I have a friend I want you to meet."

There was a banging sound as if something got knocked over in the Pullman car, then an old bespectacled man wearing a dirty striped train hat and baggy blue denim train overalls peeked out the door like a turtle from under its protective shell.

"Oh, my dear Philomena, who is that with you?" asked Beecham.

Philomena knelt down, put her arm around Daisy, and proudly shouted, "It's my traveling buddy Daisy, formerly of the Isle of Manhattan."

"I see," Beecham said as he removed his wire-rimmed glasses and cleaned them on his overalls. Then he took a long look at Daisy, as if he were sizing her up. "I've met a few of your kind in my travels across the country. You probably have the gift of speech, which means you likely also have unusual curiosity and are highly intelligent, right?"

Daisy switched her tail a little in embarrassment and asked, "How old is your Pullman car?"

Beecham tilted his head this way and that, as if to better assess Daisy, and replied, "My Hamilton Pullman car dates back to before World War II. In fact, our president back then, Franklin Delano Roosevelt, actually slept in my berth way back in 1942 while traveling the country by rail."

Daisy's fur tingled and she asked, "Are you a student of history?"

"Indeed I am, Daisy," said Beecham as he and Daisy stared at each other for what seemed like a very long time.

"Well, we must be going," Philomena said. "See ya, Beecham. You owe us a tour when we return from Noshi's place."

Daisy wasn't sure what had just taken place, but now, from the feelings she had experienced, she was even more curious about this Pullman car on the abandoned track.

As Philomena and Daisy resumed their hike, they were silent for a long time. Finally, Philomena blurted out, "What happened back there?"

Daisy stopped her hippity-hop walk and replied, "I don't know how to explain it. I just sensed that Beecham's Pullman car was like the tip of an iceberg, that whatever we were allowed to see of it was only a fraction of what was really there. I kept seeing a vision of a strange museum with many, many paintings. Does any of that make sense?"

Philomena chuckled and replied, "Did I not pick the most perceptive partner for this mission of mysteries?"

Daisy was still self-conscious about what she was feeling and thought that maybe she was just starting to really tap in to a strength she possessed that had been there to some degree all along.

Philomena asked, "Hey, do you think the changing painting in the Pink Garter Saloon and Beecham's Pullman car are connected in some way?"

Daisy smiled and said, "Great minds think alike."

As they walked side by side near the tracks leading north toward the canyon, Philomena said, "Keep your eyes open, Daisy. I usually find things in the dirt on this path."

Soon Daisy came across a piece of pottery, a shard of what had perhaps been a teacup saucer, visible as the baking sun reflected off of it. Philomena took her backpack off and, with the seriousness of a paleontologist, pulled out a magnifying glass and used it to study the shard. She concluded, "Yup, as I suspected—it's from the old El Ortiz Hotel. Back at the turn of the century there was a man named Fred Harvey who built hotels alongside the railroad, one in Lamy. The sun symbol there, with the rays of light spreading out from it, was his special design."

"What happened to the hotel?" Daisy inquired.

Philomena carefully placed the shard in the small outside pocket of her backpack and said, "Around 1945, things weren't looking so good for his hotels. People preferred to drive their cars instead of taking trains everywhere."

"How do you know so much about all this?" asked Daisy.

"My dad loves the old trains and the old hotels of that era. He says it was a different time, more gracious and gentle. According to him, that guy Harvey knew how to create an aura around his hotels. The girls who worked there were called Harvey Girls and were famous. A movie was made about them many years ago," Philomena explained.

Philomena kept her magnifying glass in her hand, knowing there might be more treasures hidden in the dirt. As if on cue, Daisy spotted another glint in the dust. "Philomena!" she shouted. "Look over there!"

As they both circled the partially visible object, Daisy pawed it out of the dirt. Then Philomena rubbed the dirt off of it and said, "It's just old bottle glass worn smooth from exposure to the sun, wind, and rain, but I love the milky gray-green color. Perfect!" Philomena declared. "I've been looking for one of these so Noshi can make a leather bracelet with it. On my hikes up to his home I love to find objects that he can make into beautiful jewelry."

"What's on the other side of the train tracks?" Daisy asked as they continued to hike and hunt for treasure.

"That's the arroyo that cuts through the canyon and follows the tracks all the way into Lamy," Philomena answered. "It's a dry creek most of the year, but sometimes water runs down it from the mountains."

"You mean like a river?" Daisy asked, with fear creeping into her voice.

"Yeah. You don't want to get caught in a flash flood out here," Philomena said.

The sun's arc was tracking a little lower in the sky as they came to the turnoff that led up the steep mountain to Noshi's home.

"Loose Caboose Lane—that's our turnoff, Daisy," announced Philomena.

As improbable as it seemed, a sad old train caboose painted fire-engine red was on a mound of dirt right in front of them. Daisy thought it looked like a cartoon come to life.

"This has been here forever. Whoever owned it left long ago," explained Philomena. "We have about a mile left, and it's uphill, Daisy. I think we should eat again and rest before we climb." Daisy agreed.

A welcome light breeze wafted through the canyon to where they sat. As Philomena rummaged in her pack to find their food, Daisy asked, "I'm really curious about your friend Noshi. What's he like?"

After taking her time chewing a big piece of beef jerky and ruminating about Daisy's question, Philomena answered, "He's a very creative artist and a unique person. He treats me like an adult. He encourages me to be adventurous. He asks me questions, and he says outrageous things and always surprises me!"

"Like what?" Daisy asked, rubbing her paws together.

"Well, the last time I saw him he told me that an angel with wings so long and heavy that they dragged behind him was watching over me. He said, 'Philomena, never try to fit in, never follow the crowd. They are always lost. Just run your own race.' Of all the people in Lamy, I think he is the most creative. He lives alone but loves it when company visits. He has no pets; he loves all animals. He's like a child, yet he's older than my dad."

Daisy asked, "How did you meet him?"

Philomena took off her sun hat, wiped her sweaty forehead, and replied, "I first met Noshi when I was hiking alone on the other side of the arroyo and came upon a raven that was circling over my head. I loved watching it swoop and turn as if it were interested in me. I was getting dizzy watching the beautiful black bird. Then I looked to my right and saw a little painting on an easel, though it seemed nobody was there. I didn't see Noshi because he was lying on his back in the dirt staring up at that bird and singing to it. That's how we met." As if to punctuate Philomena's reply, Bishop Lamy and Willa suddenly fluttered overhead.

"Are you two joining us at Noshi's this afternoon?" Philomena inquired playfully.

Right away, they circled above the two travelers then flew up the mountain. Philomena and Daisy packed up and followed them.

The climb and the heat were taking their toll on Daisy. They still had about a quarter mile to go, so Philomena decided to put Daisy on her back and carry her the rest of the way. Daisy leaned in close to Philomena and nuzzled her hair. Philomena had become a desert tour guide to Daisy, continuously pointing things out as they walked. "We're above the tree line here. Look at the view! You can see the railroad tracks below, Daisy," she exclaimed.

The sun was reflecting off the tracks far below, which stretched out to the horizon. Now walking a narrow spine of the mountain, with Daisy still on her back, Philomena pointed to a structure in the distance. "It looks like a giant rock set in the mountainside. You almost don't even see it," Daisy said.

As they approached, Philomena gently pulled Daisy off her shoulders and whispered, "Noshi told me that he built his home over thirty years ago all by himself, using only what the earth provided."

Daisy surveyed the entrance. It didn't look like a normal door; it looked like a portal. "Is Noshi the man from my dream?" she wondered. Daisy's fur again tingled as she thought about portals to strange new realities and the courage it takes to jump through them.

Two large, craggy, reddish orange rocks stood guard on either side of the entrance. The slanting afternoon light beamed partway into the corridor that led into the main structure. Suddenly, the two doves flew into the corridor side by side, ahead of Philomena and Daisy.

As Daisy stepped into the long corridor, she noted that it felt deliciously cool.

While approaching the light ahead of them, Philomena said quietly, "Noshi may be working in his studio. I don't want to surprise him."

"I think the doves have already told Noshi of our arrival," Daisy replied.

The hallway suddenly opened into an enormous, perfectly round space about a hundred feet in circumference, with two levels descending from it. Daisy took in the extraordinary sight, thinking the house looked like giant ripples of water moving out from the lowest and smallest level. Everything appeared homemade—earthy and funky. The floor was simply hard-pressed dirt. A weathered old

tree branch was attached to the wall behind them, where the doves sat watching them.

Daisy scanned the three levels. It appeared that the lowest level was for sleeping; there was an ancient pot-bellied stove in the center, with bedrolls laid out close by and a small table with what looked like a diary on top. The next, bigger level contained a hodgepodge of things strewn about, including a pottery wheel and chair, with clay littered everywhere and a jeweler's table with a dim green light streaming down on it. Daisy surmised that this must be where Noshi made jewelry.

Daisy was beginning to think that this artist was quite messy. "Maybe there is a connection between creativity and messiness!" she mused.

Philomena saw Daisy looking at the windows encir-cling half of the upper level and whispered, "They're all different. Noshi told me that he scoured every thrift store in Santa Fe to find windows that 'spoke' to him."

The windows faced due south and west, casting the-atrical shadows against the far wall in various sizes, shapes, and colors. Some were blue and others golden; some had small panes, and others large panes. The light filtering through the many colors and hues created a magical environment. Daisy said to Philomena, "The windows make this home like a kaleidoscope."

"Noshi told me once that he wanted to design a happy castle for himself. I think he succeeded," Philomena said.

Upon entering the large round space on the upper level, Daisy and Philomena saw only one thing—a large painting on a stout wooden easel, illuminated by window light flooding the space. Approaching the painting reverently and gazing at it although it was partially covered with a dirty artist's cloth, they could see enough to know it was a realistic rendering of a Native American woman. The top of the painting was still shrouded in the cloth.

"I'd be happy to show you both the rest of my painting; however, it is a work in progress, like us all," a voice boomed out.

Philomena and Daisy wheeled around to see Noshi standing in front of them.

# CHAPTER 5

"I imagine you intrepid travelers could use some food after that long hike," Noshi said.

Philomena cleared her dry throat and replied, "This is my friend Daisy from New York City. We'd love some of your special green chile tea if you have any."

Noshi looked down at Daisy and said in a comforting voice, "Tea is coming up. I also have some fabulous bizcochitos that would be an appropriate pairing."

Daisy wrinkled her nose and asked, "What?"

"They're a little like Mexican cinnamon wedding cookies, very delicious," explained Philomena.

Daisy studied the man in front of her. He appeared to be between fifty and sixty years old, slender, of an undefined ethnicity as if a citizen of the world, and had salt-and-pepper hair tightly pulled back in a ponytail. His eyes were gray-green, similar in color to the weathered glass fragment that Daisy and Philomena had found on their hike. He wore an old, tattered, blue chambray work shirt tucked messily into paint-spattered blue jeans that were held up by a pair of yellow suspenders. What stood out most was the angular quality of his face. He had high cheekbones and sharp creases, especially on the sides of his mouth. Were it not for his weathered skin and the pronounced crow's feet radiating from his eyes, he would have appeared twenty years younger.

Noshi looked penetratingly at Daisy and said, cryptically, "You are different. You have the gift."

"What gift?" Daisy asked.

"You can see what is beyond the realms of normal vision, Daisy," Noshi replied. "And your sister," he said, turning to Philomena, "also possesses extraordinary gifts. She is a throwback to a time of adventurers and dreamers, when unbounded imagination and courage were the coin of the realm."

Daisy saw Philomena's eyes begin to tear up, and then she began to shiver. Daisy jumped into Philomena's lap, hoping her touch would comfort her friend. Noshi prepared the tea and cookies.

After a time, Philomena said in a small voice, "I've always known I was different, that I didn't fit in anywhere. I always feel alone, Daisy." Philomena held her head in her hands, and Daisy could see her companion's frustrations surface.

"You've got me now," Daisy said, "and we can both be special together."

"Come to think of it, you and Noshi and me are all loners. And I think loners like other loners. Anyway, Daisy, I knew there was a reason I decided to contact you—you and I are a team."

Noshi returned with a comically tall pile of cookies and said sheepishly to Philomena, "I am sorry my words upset you. You know you are like a daughter to me, don't you? I may have chosen the wrong time to say these things to you, but please trust me when I say that the sooner you realize the gifts you possess the sooner you will fully blossom into who you are truly meant to be."

Philomena nodded in agreement and wiped the last tear away from her cheek.

"I sense we have things to discuss, so I propose, oh elevated ones," Noshi said in a funny, imperious tone, "that we converse outside on the veranda, where a very theatrical sunset is brewing. Philomena, do you remember what I told you about measuring sunset times?"

Without saying a word, Philomena raised her right arm straight out to face the low-hanging sun and stuck her thumb out sideways, facing the horizon. "One thumb, half hour; two thumbs, one hour," she recited.

"I'd say by your measurement that we have two thumbs of light left, or one hour before sunset, right?" asked Noshi. Philomena smiled and nodded, lowering her arm.

"Now I strongly suggest my two Imagination Warriors bed down at Casa Noshi tonight," continued Noshi.

Philomena looked at Daisy and said, "I agree with Noshi. Even if we left for home right now, we'd be traveling in the dark down the mountain." Turning to face Noshi, she asked, "Hey, what did you call us?"

Noshi took a sip of the spicy hot tea, leaned back in his chair, and said, "I called you Imagination Warriors. I am one, and you and Daisy are, too. You both possess the gift of knowing the truth that is revealed when looking deeply into the world. We realize that our path through this life is different from that of the vast majority of people. Philomena, you go your own way, dress your own way, and have an independent vision of yourself in the world. And, whether you realize it or not, your curiosity and imagination are the potent fuel that fires your life." Noshi took a bite of a cookie and then, focusing on Daisy, said, "You have great psychic powers and the rare ability to speak. I've only known a few animals with that gift, and they were all truly special beings. I suspect you are questioning what's going on in our little village of Lamy regarding the flow of time."

Daisy's fur felt as if an electric current was running through it as she replied, "From the moment I entered the Lamy train station I got the eerie feeling that I'd crossed a threshold between normal time and wonky time. I felt as if the normal rules about time running in only one direction did not apply here, that time here is fluid, that past and present could exist simultaneously, and that a traveler could move fluidly between the two. Possibly Lamy is the center of a time and space vortex that might be unique in the world." She looked at Philomena and added, "Philomena has put a lot of trust in my psychic abilities, and I really believe that my sixth sense about all this is accurate, as unbelievable as it sounds. Philomena has some photos to show you."

Philomena pulled the five photos she had taken in the Pink Garter Saloon out of her backpack and spread them out on the table, making sure they were in chronological order. Noshi leaned in, looking closely at the sequence.

"What was the lapse of time between the first and last picture?" Noshi inquired.

"About one week," Philomena replied.

Noshi looked at both of them intently and said, "I've known for some time that Lamy is more than it appears to be, and those chosen ones with the gift of true seeing are aware of this. I've begun to play with the idea that creativity and imagination are actually living things."

With a puzzled look, Philomena said, "I don't understand. Are you saying this painting in the saloon is alive?"

Noshi pointed back to his house and replied, "That painting in there, the one I'm currently working on, has taken on a life of its own, too. What I painted was a Native American princess wearing a golden headdress, but it's changing every day now, and I have a theory about it. Here's what I believe to be true: artists throughout time have been disruptors, transgressors, and outliers. Their job description has always been to create something out of nothing and to have it be so remarkable that when other people look at it they get the feeling that the work of art is speaking directly to them, changing the way they see the world and, eventually, changing their lives.

"That's all I did when I began the painting, fellow Imagination Warriors. But our Lamy time-space vortex is getting bigger or more intense, so that creativity and imagination are able to transcend boundaries as never before and become real things. Or maybe the changing painting has something to do with the new oil paints I found in Italy, which have an exquisite yellow pigment that I used liberally to create the crown of the princess. In any case, I have observed that my painting is transforming all by itself. The crown I've painted seemingly does not want to stay a crown but to develop golden rays of light that extend outward to the upper edge of the canvas, in much the same way the teepees and grass in your photos of the painting in the Pink Garter Saloon have changed on their own."

"So if these paintings are coming alive, what are we supposed to do?" Philomena asked.

"Good question, Imagination Warrior," Noshi said with a smile.

"I think time is porous here; it ebbs and flows," Daisy blurted out before she could think, but the look from both Noshi and Philomena gave her the confidence to tell everything she was feeling. "I think Beecham's Pullman car is one of those places where time has the freedom to run both ways, and I believe he knows it."

Philomena observed Noshi doing something she'd seen him do countless times that always amused her. He was massaging his temples with his right thumb and middle finger as if coaxing deep thoughts from his mind. Eventually Noshi said, "Fellow Imagination Warriors, New Mexico's high desert is a wondrous and magical place; to my thinking, it's unique in the world. At the risk of overwhelming you both, I feel it's time, given the mysteries that currently swirl about us, to prepare ourselves psychically for the journey in which we've chosen to engage. I'd hoped to introduce this phenomenon to you, Philomena, when you became ten years old, but now I realize that it can't wait any longer. Since the sunset is just minutes away, we must make haste slowly. Daisy, you and Philomena are very old souls, and I have confidence that you both will be informed and inspired by what I'm about to show you." Philomena and Daisy glanced at each other with a look of both trepidation and anticipation.

The sun was a half-thumb up from the horizon, and the landscape was becoming transformed as long shadows swept over earth and tree and rock. Noshi had quickly gone back into his house and grabbed three old wool blankets that he tied together and then strapped onto his back. Noshi now pointed to a plateau about a hundred meters away and said, "We must get to that spot before the sun sets."

They walked quickly, following Noshi along the spine of the mountain. All around them the mountain dropped off abruptly at the sides of the path. Daisy was amazed to see Noshi walk with an effortless, graceful gait as if he were weightless. By the time they reached their destination, the light had turned from a harsh yellow-gold to a muted pastel purple.

"Here," Noshi said. They formed a circle facing one another, and sat cross-legged on a flat patch of earth overlooking a wide expanse of the mountains that had taken on a dusty purple light. The sun was balanced perfectly on the horizon's edge.

Noshi wrapped the wool blankets around Philomena and Daisy and said, in a serious voice, "Be still, it's almost time."

Daisy's mind was racing, and her senses were crackling like fireworks. She forcibly focused on the warmth and weight of the blanket to be fully present in the moment. The winds were kicking up now that the sun had set below the mountains, and she could hear them howl in the low brush that grew all around them.

Daisy and Philomena faced Noshi and looked into his eyes for some sign of what was to come. Daisy then snuck a peek at Philomena, who already appeared to be in some sort of trance-like state.

"Focus your vision upward to the sky," Noshi told them.

The sky faded to yellow at the horizon, then further up deep blue and purple.

"It's beginning," whispered Noshi.

Then something unexplainable appeared in the sky above them. Silvery filaments of light began to drop down from the multitudes of stars now shining overhead. Daisy watched in awe as the spidery filaments continued their descent to earth, unable to believe what she was seeing.

Entranced, Daisy looked toward Philomena for some kind of confirmation that they were seeing the same thing. Philomena looked back, spellbound, and nodded slowly. The silver threads were now touching all parts of the visible earth—the mountains, valleys, and even the

cities far in the distance. Then suddenly the filaments of light that had touched down on the earth were all connected with one another, like a map of airline routes crisscrossing the globe. Time stood still for them as the glowing filaments connected with everything alive: all natural things, all man-made things, oceans and rivers, deserts and jungles.

During the walk back to Noshi's house, in a hushed and weighty voice he said, "Always remember this evening, Imagination Warriors. What you both witnessed in the heavens and on the earth was proof beyond a shadow of doubt that we are all interconnected. Everything that exists is held in a kind of web, whose size is unknowable and unfathomable. The most important things are the invisible things. Those who have the gift of true perception, as you both do, have the ability to see and feel the invisible things. At your peril, never forget what has transpired this evening. It was your preparation for things to come—the invisible things."

Daisy knew deep in her soul that the three of them now shared something so profound that they would be bound together all their days by their experience this night.

# CHAPTER 6

Noshi had them walk in single file behind him as they navigated the narrow mountain path back to his house in the inky dark night. They did not speak, but Daisy's mind was churning with thoughts and feelings. She was still processing a vast ocean of experiences since her arrival in Lamy the day before, although it felt like she'd been there for at least a year. She thought to herself, "Are we living in the same dimension as other people right now? Do the people in Michael's dining car know about any of this? Is this the celestial phenomenon we saw connected to the sense of porous time I could feel in Beecham's Pullman car?"

After they arrived at Noshi's house, he fired up the stove, heated some more green chile tea, and spread out three bedrolls close to the comforting heat. Daisy's cold and bone-tired little body welcomed the healing warmth. Before she drifted off to sleep, she began to question her perceptions, thinking, "Did Noshi somehow orchestrate the celestial phenomenon for us? If we are all connected, but only a few people on the earth know this, what does it mean? If we are now living in another dimension, am I still who I am? One thing is for sure: New Mexico is definitely a weird place. Nothing like this ever happens in New York City."

The next morning Daisy awoke disoriented in the dim light of Noshi's house. The lack of right angles and the different levels and darkness made the place feel even more like a spaceship traveling through the immense void of time and space. "I wonder if this is an example of thinking like an Imagination Warrior," she asked herself. As she slowly got her bearings, she realized that she was the only one awake and the sun had not yet risen.

The events of the previous night made the idea that they were somehow time travelers and that Lamy was the center of a time "ripple" believable to her. The mysteries were piling up now. "Are the painting at the Pink Garter Saloon, Noshi's painting, and Beecham's Pullman car somehow connected?" she wondered. While these mysteries seemed challenging, Daisy felt as though she was destined to solve them. In the silence of the early morning, she simply allowed thoughts to come to her, trusting they would reveal information to guide her and her fellow Imagination Warriors. In time, a provocative premise surfaced. She thought to herself, "What is the common denominator in all these occurrences? It's us, the Imagination Warriors. Could it be that simply imagination, along with the focused power to wield it, is the answer? Is the journey we find ourselves on meant for the very few gifted ones who can see into other dimensions due to the power of imagination?"

Slowly, as the light came up, suffusing the circular space with an eerie orange glow, Daisy became aware of all the books strewn about. She suppressed a little laugh as she thought to herself, "Noshi is messy, but he's very well read." Wandering over to Noshi's newest painting, she reflected, "Imagine how fabulous it must be to make a living creating things from your imagination!"

As Daisy tentatively approached the painting, her instincts told her to be very still and sort of sneak up on it. She stopped about five feet away. The painting on the easel towered above her, at a height of about six feet. The upper portion of the painting was still shrouded by the cloth, but some of the Native princess's headdress and face were visible. Noshi had painted the princess with haunting gold eyes, a headdress of nine feathers, and a necklace of seven pearls that made the girl look like royalty. She felt the painting should be entitled *The Native Princess*. Daisy had the distinct feeling that this young girl was on some sort of important mission involving responsibility for other people and that she had maturity and wisdom. In a strange way, although she was about fourteen years old and a bit taller the Native princess reminded her of Philomena. But Philomena would never wear the white flowing dress that Noshi had painted for his princess. Daisy noted that there was a fierce warrior quality to her face and her stance. Something else she noticed for the first time was Noshi's signature on the bottom right of the painting. But the most amazing thing she noticed was the way the golden rays now extended as far as the edge of the canvas.

As the sun rose above the mountains to the east, making Noshi's house look less like a scary spaceship, Daisy heard Philomena stirring on the lower level. When Philomena joined her, Daisy whispered, "The golden rays have reached the edge of the canvas! What happens now?"

"We've got to wake up Noshi," Philomena said with urgency.

Philomena shouted to Noshi, who was still asleep on the lower level, "Noshi, your painting changed again!"

"I figured it would. But it can wait until we've had some java," he said to them, pulling his hair back into a tight ponytail.

When they reconvened for breakfast at his veranda table, Philomena asked, "What should we do, Noshi?"

Noshi sipped his coffee slowly and replied, "I propose that after breakfast we three intrepid Imagination Warriors sit directly in front of my painting and see what happens."

"That will be interesting," Daisy said. Turning toward Philomena, she added, "Oh, by the way, show Noshi what we found on our hike yesterday."

Philomena reached into her backpack and said to Noshi, smiling, "I thought you could use this fragment of glass. The color reminded me of your eyes."

Noshi was visibly touched and accepted her gift graciously. "This is very interesting glass. The center part is clear, and the edges are more opaque," he said, turning the fragment over and over in his hands. "You know, when you go digging I see your father's passion in you, Philomena," he added.

After breakfast, Noshi placed three chairs directly in front of his painting. He then removed the cloth from the top. Daisy and Philomena stared in awe at the Native princess with her crown of feathers and piercing gaze.

"Okay, let's be quiet and still, and hopefully we'll get to the bottom of this situation," Noshi said in a business-like fashion.

They sat and stared for what seemed like forever with the light streaming through the stained-glass windows and dancing across Noshi's earthen walls, casting beautiful tones. Eventually, Philomena said in an exasperated voice, "Nothing is happening!" After her outburst, Philomena settled into a meditative state. She then looked over at Daisy and Noshi, who were both still and silent.

Daisy imagined she saw the feathers in the princess's crown begin to vibrate and radiate a golden ethereal light toward the upper corners of the canvas. Suddenly all nine of the golden rays that emanated from the princess's crown now reached out past the painting, increasing in size and intensity.

"It's changing!" Daisy shouted. At that moment, the golden beams reached up and struck Noshi's ceiling.

Immediately, Philomena, Noshi, and Daisy were physically pulled into the painting by some irresistible gravitational force. As they crossed the threshold that

had been the painting's surface, everything grew dark. They were completely disoriented—there was motion but no sound, no way to get their bearings or determine their location.

"I'm scared, Noshi," cried Philomena as she instinctively clutched Daisy to her chest.

"We appear to be on a strange journey. At least we are all together and not hurt," Noshi replied.

Soon they heard very faint sounds, like a radio broadcast, getting louder and softer. Then they heard a swooshing sound, as if air was being forcibly pushed through something, followed by the sensation of warm, humid wind on their bodies. Daisy recalled being on a subway platform with Mrs. Z in New York City one summer, feeling the oncoming rush of moist air when a train approached the station.

"What should we do, Noshi?" Philomena asked, insistently.

"Let's continue to listen. It might give us a clue about where we are...or when we are."

"Noshi, do you think that because we are now Imagination Warriors we were able to enter your painting?" asked Daisy.

"The power of the imagination is as boundless as the imaginer's ability to dream," he answered cryptically.

In the distance, they heard the faint sounds of drums, babies crying, people talking, something flapping in the wind, rain falling hard on the ground, and booming claps of thunder. Daisy remarked, "It sounds like a party when you are far away and cannot hear individual voices."

The darkness faded into a half-light a little like moonlight, with dusky blue, gray, and silver hues. The faint sounds stopped, and the rushing, warm air diminished.

"Where are we, Noshi?" asked Philomena.

"I believe we are between here and there, now and before, and maybe even a time yet to be," he said mysteriously. "It seems that my painting, for unknown reasons, is a portal, and we're being transported somewhere. What I find so fascinating is the concept that a work of art could actually take us on such a journey!"

"Here we are, traveling through thunder, darkness, moonlight, time, and space to wherever, and only you, my friend Noshi, could be so philosophical about it!" Philomena said.

Soon the three travelers felt a gradual change in the frequency of the sounds and level of light, as if everything were speeding up. They now experienced a kind of strobe effect, like moving through a tunnel at an incredible speed with lights flashing, sounds louder and harsher, and increased wind speed, almost as though a storm were approaching. Then everything stopped, except for a hard, cold rain pelting them.

Daisy saw an opening in front of them and became aware that they were in a teepee with rain sheeting from a flap blowing wildly in the wind. "We are in a teepee. I know them from reading western novels," she said in a calm voice.

"Incredible. I've always wanted to paint a teepee. They've always struck me as sailboats anchored to the earth. Their shapes are wonderful to render, and they catch the light in poetic ways," Noshi said.

"I don't believe this. You guys are talking about art and teepees, and we have a situation here!" Philomena replied in an exasperated voice.

It was getting cold, and they began to shiver as the rain continued. Even so, Daisy decided to move to the opening in the teepee, knowing how wet she might become. "I'm curious to see where we are," she said. Philomena and Noshi moved behind her.

Suddenly, there was a scary thunderclap overhead. As the three travelers peeked out, the cold rain lashed their faces and the wind blew so hard it began moving the teepee back and forth. Daisy had a disturbing thought: "What if our imaginations are not always benevolent and happy? What if our imaginations access darker visions that lie deep within us?" Daisy tried to believe, instead, that her imagination and those of her friends were pre-dictable and positive.

An ominous charcoal-colored cloud was now moving quickly across the sky in their direction. "Noshi, I think the storm is getting worse. We need to find shelter. Over there is a tall rock and maybe some shelter," shouted Philomena.

They began walking through tall, wet grass that was swaying wildly in the wind. Philomena was carrying Daisy, trying to lift her above the blades of grass now whipping their faces. All of Daisy's senses were alive seeing this world unfold, and she thought to herself, "I'm almost dizzy watching those vivid green grasses move from side to side like a ballet under the charcoal-colored sky that looks angry as it threatens us."

They worked their way through the last stand of tall grasses and quickly ducked under the large overhanging rock, which offered better shelter than the teepee. As they huddled together to stay warm, Daisy asked, "Do you recognize that teepee?"

Philomena's mouth dropped open, and she shouted, "It's one of the teepees in the old painting that I photographed in the saloon!"

The three of them took a visual inventory of the scene before their eyes. "The grasses look the same, and even the boulder that the warrior was crouching on is probably this boulder we're under right now," Daisy added.

Noshi started to massage his temples as though he were trying to get his brain primed for some serious thinking. "It seems we are living in the Pink Garter Saloon painting, not in the exact moment that the picture depicts but in a time a little before or after, because the Native American man is not perched on this boulder right now," Noshi reasoned.

"That makes sense. The only teepee left is the one we came through. But what happened to the other teepees and the warrior?" asked Daisy.

"Good question, Daisy," said Philomena.

A sly smile slowly played across Daisy's face. "I wonder if anyone is looking at the painting in the Pink Garter Saloon right now and seeing us," she said. Philomena and Noshi smiled at the idea.

After a while the wind and rain stopped. "Maybe there's a clue in the teepee," said Noshi. They decided to walk back to the teepee they had originally entered.

As they traversed the field of tall grasses, Noshi mused, "This is extraordinary, fellow Imagination Warriors. Here we are breathing and walking in a painting, smelling the sweet wet air and feeling the tickle of raindrops on our cool skin. To my eyes, the colors seem so vivid and alive! I'd love to know what painting technique was used to achieve this effect!"

Daisy and Philomena chuckled at Noshi's preoccupation with painting techniques at such a time.

They approached the teepee with trepidation. Again Philomena picked Daisy up in her arms protectively. Noshi pushed the flap of the teepee aside, and they entered, only to be confronted with another painting set on an easel!

"Why didn't we see this before?" asked Philomena.

"Because we were so focused on looking out the opening in the teepee and feeling the rain that we never thought to look behind us," replied Noshi.

"Another possible reason is that our collective imaginations only 'saw' the teepees from the outside, as they were depicted in the painting in the Pink Garter Saloon," said Daisy.

The new painting appeared to be roughly the same size as Noshi's painting. The subject was a large, rectangular room dominated by a central table with wooden stairs surrounding it and a doorway visible behind it.

"Look at the ceiling," Noshi said to Daisy. "Those are large vigas, the kind of beams we have in New Mexico."

Drawing closer to the painting with Daisy held close to her chest, Philomena declared, "It looks like a hotel room. See the rug under the table? Its pattern is very southwestern." The pattern on the light gray rug looked like a stairway ascending and descending. The walls of the room were a warm white color, and set all around the room were wooden chairs.

"Everything looks old, Noshi," Philomena said.

"Didn't you tell me about an old hotel that existed many years ago by the railroad tracks?" Daisy asked.

Philomena nodded, then exclaimed, "It's the El Ortiz Hotel! Listening to my dad describe every detail of that old hotel really brought it alive for me."

Daisy added, "Your imagination has brought it alive for us, as well."

"The light is sublime in this room. Look at the windows on either side of the table. There's no direct light source, and yet the painter captured an exquisite quality of light. The light filtering through the curtains gives the whole room a golden glow so that the painting almost breathes! I'd love to know who the creator of this work is," observed Noshi.

Looking frustrated, Philomena said, "But we've moved from one painting to another and still don't know where we are or how to get home. I don't know about you guys, but I'd sure like to see something familiar—my bed, for instance. This is exhausting."

Now it was Daisy who gave encouragement to her friend, saying, "But it's incredibly exciting how we seem to be riding our imaginations in a shared dream. And for once I can use the full potential of my special gifts for all of us, not just for predicting pedestrian traffic."

# CHAPTER 7

G rady managed to sneak into the Pink Garter Saloon just before closing time. He then scouted out a small utility closet toward the back of the bathroom, where he stood silently waiting for everyone to leave the saloon and the doors to be locked. He had brought a flashlight, gloves, and strong rope, knowing that the large painting would be heavy.

Grady had never stolen anything before in his life, but there was something mesmerizing about the painting, and the fact that Philomena seemed obsessed with it made it all the more enticing. In the darkness of the small closet, he reflected on his life. "What have I accomplished so far? And why is it so hard to find things that make me happy? Everything feels like a struggle; I hate shopping and making dinner for everyone each night. I always feel that Llama Rama is laughing at me, that he'd live my life in a better way if given the opportunity to be a human."

He let a good amount of time go by before venturing out of the closet. Only a few lights had been left on, so it was very dark in the saloon, especially in the corner where the mysterious painting hung. As his flashlight darted around, finally illuminating the large painting, Grady had the oddest feeling that something was different about it, though he'd only glanced at it when he'd snuck up on Philomena. He moved very close to the painting and flashed a beam of light on the background where the three teepees stood. He took a deep breath and thought to himself, "I feel relaxed and almost happy being in a dark, calm place and looking at this painting, with nobody telling me to do anything. I wonder if meditating is like this?"

A moment later he thought he sensed movement in the upper left part of the picture, where the artist had depicted a stormy sky. Unbelievably, a dark cloud appeared to be moving from that portion of the sky at a glacially slow pace, finally settling over the teepees.

"No wonder Philly was taking photographs," Grady thought. He continued to watch in amazement as the cloud hovering menacingly above the teepees opened up and deposited an almost opaque sheet of rain onto them. Grady was spellbound by the slow-motion meteorological ballet playing out on this magical canvas in front of him.

Noshi enthusiastically declared, "I feel as though I've suddenly received a PhD in art. We are entering works of art—living, breathing works of art—and seeing the colors of the world as if for the first time!"

Philomena looked at Noshi and said, with a raised eyebrow, "I'm really glad you're enjoying the artwork, but what about our dire situation?"

Noshi could see he was being mocked. "The creed of an Imagination Warrior is to break free, to be unbounded by the conventions of life. A life well-lived demands the courage to make a leap of faith, demonstrating the fluidity of thought and action needed in the face of adversity and challenge! We three find ourselves in such a situation right now," he instructed.

Philomena looked at Noshi lovingly and shouted, "Yes, Imagination Warriors we are!"

Now something was happening to the painting of the hotel room. "It's getting larger and then smaller, as if breathing," said Daisy, wondering if their collective heightened anticipation was causing this phenomenon.

Immediately, the edges of the painting expanded beyond the contours of the canvas and enveloped the three travelers. They now experienced a disorienting sensation of being suspended in darkness yet also moving. They had entered the painting and were in transit once again.

"Look up," Noshi said in a hushed voice. They stared up at a kaleidoscope of thousands of portals—possibly entry and exit points to other realities, apparently accessed from myriad other paintings—all seemingly connected by ghostly, narrow bridges only faintly visible. "My Imagination Warrior sense tells me that our destination lies along the path we currently find ourselves on," Noshi said reassuringly.

They seemed to be traveling on one of the spectral bridges. Looking down, they saw that a narrow, nearly invisible path had formed beneath them like a ghostly apparition. Daisy was again reminded of Grand Central Station, with train tracks from all parts of the country meeting at its central hub. There are so many bridges, and they're all different," she said in awe.

Philomena looked up and then down, becoming dizzy at the sight of the vast system of bridges crisscrossing above and below them. "Look there!" she shouted excitedly, pointing at one of the spectral bridges disappearing. "It went into a doorway, probably into another reality. Can you imagine the possibilities?"

Daisy was amazed at the interdimensional portals, seemingly running on forever into dark space, some terminating at faint portals. Her fur tingled when she thought about all the gifted beings, like themselves, who must be generating new worlds with the power of focused imagination. "It's all so alive. I see new pathways forming and old ones dying, bridges falling into nothingness for lack of structure, and others being created in an instant and then disappearing into doorways!" she said.

As the spectral structures retreated behind the three travelers, they experienced darkness on their bridge.

For the first time since the beginning of their journey, Philomena felt deep loneliness without her mom and dad. Although priding herself on being strong and independent, she now felt untethered from all she knew. She was forced to confront the fact that her welfare depended on the actions of her two traveling companions and not hers alone. She took comfort in knowing that she could not have chosen two better friends to journey with into the unknown. And she thought that just maybe it was a good thing to be a part of something bigger than yourself.

"Listen, the sounds are coming back again," Daisy said.

They heard the faint clanking of silverware, muted talking and laughter, and the screech of a train's metal wheels.

"Now the lights are coming up again," Daisy said. They were entering the part of the transit where they had experienced the eerie moonlight effect. Then, as before, the wind died down, the sounds stopped, and the strobe lighting appeared.

Noshi said, "We are in the final stage of transit."

When they assessed their surroundings, they realized that they had been deposited in a dark corridor with yet another painting hanging on the wall in the dim light behind them. "Looks like a painting of a dark cave—not very inviting," Daisy said.

"Something about this looks familiar to me. I don't think it's a cave," Philomena remarked.

"Even this painting exhibits a startling command of the color palette. Look at the beautiful striations in the colors of the rock and the flecks of greenish turquoise set within them," Noshi said, admiringly.

"If this is the El Ortiz Hotel, I'll bet the large room in the painting is around the corner," Philomena whispered.

They walked the length of the dark corridor and came to an adjoining hallway, which was much brighter. Philomena smiled, recognizing the building, and said, "Yes, this is the El Ortiz Hotel. I wish I could share this moment with my dad, like he always shared things he loved with me."

As the three travelers stood at the entrance to the vast room, Noshi observed, "Very commodious. I love the warm white plaster walls and the way the golden western light floods in through those pale yellow drapes."

In the center of the room was a large chandelier that hung ceremoniously over the community table. Daisy said, "It all looks really gracious in an old-time way. I'd love to chat with the people who used to gather around the table."

Philomena gently told Daisy, "Sweetie, back in this time, around 1930, folks might be a little alarmed by a talking cat."

Noshi chimed in, "Yes, I think we should keep a low profile. We may already look a little strange to people of this time."

Feeling adventurous once again, Philomena declared, "I want to go outside and see what 1930 looks like."

Grady hadn't counted on the painting being as heavy as it was. He struggled to lift it off its stout wire hanger, eventually managing to remove it from the wall and slide it along the saloon's wooden floor toward the entrance.

It was dark outside. He peeked out the front door to make sure no one was around, then, leaving the painting just inside the saloon, he ran to his parents' old Toyota pickup truck, which he'd parked by Michael's dining car across the dirt road. He pulled the truck up as close to the saloon's entrance as possible, hoisted the painting into it, and, as an afterthought, guiltily swiped at his tire tracks in the dirt with his boots.

"Imagination Warriors are a fearless breed. Let's investigate our village," said Noshi optimistically.

Getting worried about their location, Daisy asked, "Don't you think we should try to return to our time through the painting portal? What if someone moves the painting and we can't find our way back?"

"I never thought of that possibility, Daisy," said Philomena.

"Daisy, I wouldn't worry about that happening," said Noshi in a reassuring tone. "The painting's probably been hanging in that dark hallway for years, and everybody's forgotten about it. Besides, we're just beginning to discover how powerful our collective imaginations are."

As they exited the El Ortiz Hotel, they were assaulted by the sights and sounds of a time long gone. Old-time cars with straight-up windshields and fat whitewall tires were beeping *aahhhuuggaa* and stirring up the desert dirt as they passed by. Philomena was fascinated by the women in stylish long dresses and hats that looked like halos.

Noshi eyed a general store across the dirt road and led the other awestruck Imagination Warriors in that direction. "I believe that's the old—I mean the present—Pfluegers General Store," he said.

"That sure is a funny name for a store," Philomena commented.

"Pflueger was a German immigrant who came to Lamy before the turn of the century and opened this very store," Noshi said. "Let's go there now."

Philomena thought to herself that Old Lamy looked and sounded louder and busier than the Lamy she knew. She scooped up Daisy and stayed close to Noshi as they dodged the tall cars with enormous headlights and swoopy fenders on their way to the general store.

It was now midafternoon, and the sun was beginning the second half of its graceful arc to the western horizon. Philomena thrust out her left thumb toward the sun as she held Daisy safely in her right hand, squinted, and discovered that it was about three in the afternoon.

"I sense that something important awaits us in the old general store," Daisy proclaimed.

# CHAPTER 8

As they approached the general store, Daisy had the same feeling she'd had when her train had first entered the Lamy station. She whispered to Noshi and Philomena, "There is something mysterious about this store. My sixth sense tells me it is not entirely there."

"What do you mean, Daisy?" asked Philomena.

"We all see this building, apparently made of wood and metal, but I feel that it's an in-between place not necessarily in our dimension. All I know is that there is an important piece of the puzzle in there and we must find it," Daisy said with conviction, her fur tingling.

Noshi guided them across the street and said, "As before, let's not call attention to ourselves."

Philomena quipped, "Yeah, that'll be easy."

As they entered the store through its large wooden doors painted a faded white, Philomena gently placed

Daisy on the weathered plank floor. It was a bustling place stocked with all sorts of things. Daisy noticed large burlap sacks of grains and apples in metal tins on the floor. Noshi and Philomena surveyed the various goods neatly placed in wooden cubbies against the walls: toothpaste, candy bars, straw hats, cigars and cigarettes, even gardening tools. Daisy noticed that the labels looked slightly familiar but old.

Daisy then spotted a small painting leaning against the bottom of the counter to her right. Her senses were on high alert as she moved toward the little painting. Noshi watched her as she sniffed it.

"Dear child, are you buying supplies for a camping trip?" asked a rotund woman standing beside Philomena.

"No, we're looking for some cat food for my cat," Philomena replied. "I always dress like this, ma'am," she added, looking down at her dusty cargos.

The woman gave her a dismissive look and turned her attention to Noshi and Daisy, who were still examining the painting. Anticipating questions, she offered, "It's just a study for a bigger painting by the artist, but may never be finished."

"Why?" asked Noshi.

"He ran out one day looking very upset and disappeared into the hotel, and I haven't seen him since. I leave this picture here just to see if anyone might be interested in buying it," the woman answered.

Daisy, eyeing it more closely, noted light blasting out of the building's doorway, which looked like a giant, old-fashioned keyhole. The building was painted a shocking shade of pink.

Noshi carefully picked up the painting and held it close to his face. "Can you tell me about the artist?" he inquired.

"He's a funny sort. He used to come and go," the woman answered, pushing her spectacles up the bridge of her nose. "He has shown up here from time to time and sold us his paintings. I never got the sense that he really needed money, though. I always thought he came from some sort of European royalty, given how he carried himself—very proper and formal in an Old World kind of way."

"And what is his name, ma'am?" Noshi asked.

The woman pushed her glasses up again and said, "His name is Mr. Temporani. I don't know his first name." Daisy's fur tingled when she heard the name.

"Does he live here in Lamy?" Noshi pressed.

"All I know is that he comes and goes and that he also did the painting in the El Ortiz Hotel across the street," said the woman.

"The one in the dark corridor?" Philomena asked.

The woman's attention was clearly wandering as she had people in line wanting to buy things, but she managed to answer in a clipped voice, as she turned away from them, "Yes, that one."

Noshi motioned silently to his Imagination Warriors to move to a quiet corner of the general store and sit around an old, low table that was probably used for stacking goods before they were placed on shelves. "I recognize the subject of this painting, and maybe you do, too," Noshi said, looking at Philomena. "I believe it's the Scottish Rite Masonic Temple in Santa Fe; its archi-tecture is unmistakable."

"Hey, I think you're right, Noshi. Mom and I used to drive by it and wonder what was inside and why it was painted that weird pink color," Philomena said.

Noshi continued, "Let's take a little inventory, Imagi-nation Warriors." He placed his thumb and middle finger on either side of his eyebrows, gently massaged them, then said, "We have identified two paintings, and maybe more, by this mysterious Mr. Temporani."

Daisy jumped in to say, "I'll bet he also made the Native American painting we fell into."

Noshi and Philomena nodded in agreement.

"We need to investigate the Scottish Rite Masonic Temple. I think some of our questions will be answered if we can get in there," Noshi suggested. "Somehow, we must buy that painting. The lady said it was a study—I do those all the time, and I would not value my studies highly. Perhaps we can offer something for it, though we don't have much."

"The piece of worn glass, which looks almost like a gemstone!" suggested Daisy.

People in the store had begun to stare at the three trav-elers sitting on the floor, so they had to act quickly. Noshi dove into his right pants pocket and found seventy-five cents and the beautiful piece of green-gray glass that Philomena had given him. "This may just do the trick, fellow Imagination Warriors," he said hopefully.

Noshi stepped forward, displaying the glass piece between his thumb and index finger, and said to the woman, "I might be willing to take that study off your hands if you're amenable." He held the glass piece up then turned it slowly as if it were a diamond catching light through its faceted glass surfaces. "I happened to notice that your painting appears incomplete. Had the artist intended to finish it?" he asked coyly.

The woman pushed her errant reading glasses back in place and saw that indeed the tall steps leading to the building's keyhole-shaped entrance were not fully painted yet. "Well, It Is a study, after all," she offered. "I might have a buyer coming in later to look at it. What do you have in mind? Surely you don't mean to trade the painting for that piece of glass, do you?" she bargained.

"This is genuine Lamy arroyo river glass, worn smooth by sun, sand, and flood. Personally, I think it would make a beguiling necklace centerpiece since it almost looks like a gemstone and its color is magnificent," Noshi replied theatrically, turning the glass in his fingers so it caught the last rays of golden sunlight.

To reinforce Noshi's offer, Philomena added, "We would give your painting a good home and throw in seventy-five cents!"

The woman held the glass up close to her face to inspect it. "All right, straight trade. The glass and your seventy-five cents for that painting. Now be gone—I've got paying customers waiting behind you," she said, arching an eyebrow at them.

Noshi gently plunked down the glass piece and the money, then quickly picked up the painting, not giving the woman a chance to second-guess her decision.

As they left the general store, Philomena could tell that something was nagging at Noshi. "What is it? You made a great deal for us back there," she said supportively.

"We gave her three quarters from our time. If anyone looks at the dates, we'll have questions to answer," Noshi said gravely.

Philomena said, "Nobody ever looks at money anymore. We'll be fine."

Tucking the little painting securely under his right arm, with renewed energy Noshi declared, "I'm sure this man Temporani holds the key to our returning home, and this little painting will help us get there."

Just then Philomena impulsively glanced up the hill on which her family's house would be built in about eighty years. There on the hill sat the majestic pine tree, though in this earlier time it was quite a bit smaller.

Daisy leaned into Philomena's leg, knowing what her friend was feeling, and said emphatically, "That tree is just waiting for your house and the laughter and love you will fill it with."

Philomena's eyes teared up as she bent down to hug her good friend. "I feel so alone right now, Daisy—like a ship being tossed around in a dangerous storm. I want to go home and hug my mom and dad and jump in my bed and go to sleep. But my parents haven't even been born yet in this time." Philomena knelt down in the dirt road and began to cry softly.

Daisy jumped into her lap and softly purred, "You are not alone, Philomena, and until we all return home we're your family."

Noshi knelt down and caressed the top of Philomena's head, saying, "You keep it all together so well, my dear, that sometimes you even fool me. I know the real you, the one who loves to share her discoveries with friends, who loves to feel connected not just admired, who doesn't always want to walk alone. That's the one I'm talking to now. Philomena, you are actually not a loner but just persnickety about who you spend time with. Daisy and I are honored to count you as a friend and fellow Imagination Warrior in good standing."

# CHAPTER 9

Grady had hidden the painting under an old plastic tarp in the bed of his parents' pickup truck and parked the truck far from his house, under a canopy of trees for protection in the unlikely chance of rain. Transporting the painting to a remote location would involve Llama Rama and a climb up Cerro Colorado, the local mountain that overlooked Lamy.

His parents, who were starting an import-export business in Santa Fe, always got home late and too tired to make dinner for everyone, so Grady was routinely enlisted to help cook. And today, as often occurred, his younger sister MacCaully was with his parents because they didn't have money to spend on a babysitter. Stepping into the kitchen, Grady put a big pot of water on the stove to cook pasta, sliced and buttered some Italian bread, then shoved it in the oven. As he waited for the water to boil, he wondered why he was so obsessed with Philomena. Maybe it was because she seemed to be the center of attention in Lamy, loved by everyone. And she seemed to have everything—a beautiful home, a cool mom, even her own signature look. Now he would feel special and important because he had a secret he could share with her: the living painting.

As the water began to simmer, Grady reflected more on his life in Lamy. He thought to himself, "I'd just about trade my life here for anybody else's anywhere." Then as the water reached a rolling boil, he had a thought that seemed farfetched yet intriguing: "Is the painting magical, and could I enter it? Have Philomena and that cat already found their way into it? I'd ditch this sad, boring little life of mine for even just a sliver of magic and mystery, and the chance to feel special like Philomena."

"Grady, we're home, and we're tired and starving!" yelled his mom as the rest of his family entered the house.

"Mac wants something pronto. Whatcha got that's fast?" his father asked.

Grady had to suppress any more fantasies about a better future as he returned to his duties of preparing and serving his family's dinner.

The next morning at sunrise, Grady removed the painting from the pickup truck and placed it on Rama's back, securing it with strong ropes around his belly. Rama was an old soul who had seen a great deal during his numerous reincarnations, which involved as many as one hundred lives before this current one. Some nights, MacCaully could hear Rama shouting commands and crying out in his sleep. She always felt protective of him, knowing deep down that he'd not been lucky in most of his previous lives.

Grady tightened the tarp around the painting to prevent anyone from seeing it. All the while, Rama thought to himself, "The fates, they are a fickle lot. This callous young man knows absolutely nothing about me or the lives I've led. What would he do if he knew that I was once a general sending young men his age into battle? What would he think if he knew I was once a statesman and a thief?"

"Where are you going, Grady?" asked MacCaully suspiciously, as she stepped outside and wiped the sleep from her eyes.

"None of your business," he replied in a surly voice, annoyed that his younger sister had woken up early.

"Dad says bring food and water for Rama, and don't forget Rama's eyeglasses and the rope to attach them. He needs them for reading when the light is dim," said MacCaully, acting like the older of the two.

"Yeah, I know, Sis, I got his glasses. I'm just gonna camp out a night. Gotta get away for a while and try to get my head straight," he said.

"What's under the cover?" she asked, moving closer to Rama and touching the tarp.

"I'm delivering a glass table up Loose Caboose Lane and then camping on the mountaintop. I can't take the pickup; it's too steep."

"Oh, okay. Remember to treat Rama good and make sure he is fed and can use his eyeglasses," MacCaully reminded him, still feeling suspicious.

Grady started walking away and said over his shoulder, "I know, Mac. See you tomorrow morning."

When MacCaully had struggled with writing and math in school, Rama would quietly help her. Knowing that her llama was very smart, she'd had a pair of custom reading glasses made for him. She would laugh at the sight of him wearing them on his long furry nose, with the rope strapped around his strong neck. Rama liked MacCaully because she always treated him with kindness and respect. With Grady, things were different. Rama rarely used his gift of speech in Grady's presence, not trusting him. But this day Rama knew Grady was unhappy with his life and needed someone with him, so Rama decided to go where Grady led him.

Grady headed for Cerro Colorado, a five-hundred-foot-high mountain shaped like a pup tent, with a narrow spine and steep sides of talus rock, that looked down on Lamy. He often climbed the mountain to be alone, but this day he also planned to hide the painting. He scanned the sky apprehensively. "Weather's changing quickly," Grady said to Rama as they walked across the east-west railroad tracks. Rama sniffed the air and knew something was brewing.

MacCaully tailed Grady to the Lamy Train Station and hid behind one of its faded yellow pillars, watching her brother and Rama head to Cerro Colorado. The wind picked up and was blowing dirt and debris sideways. The people waiting on the train platform scurried into the station to take cover from the fierce winds.

"You ought to be seeking shelter. Haboob coming," said someone behind MacCaully.

She whirled around to see Wyler, astride Loco, looking down on her. "What's a haboob?" she shouted into the wind.

Wyler scanned the ominous northern sky, which had grown a dark charcoal gray. "A destructive desert storm that scours the earth," he answered.

MacCaully observed that Grady and Rama had begun the steep climb up the talus rock of the mountain, although the wind whipping against her face made it difficult to see.

"We gotta get you outta here, Mac," Wyler said with urgency. "Hop up here and I'll take you home."

She looked back at the mountain. Grady and Rama had almost disappeared in the flying sand. "No," MacCaully said. "See my brother climbing Cerro Colorado with Rama? We need to follow them!"

Wyler squinted in the direction of the mountain. "What does Grady think he's doing? They're really exposed up there," he said, frowning. "And this storm's comin' in fast. We have about ten good minutes before all hell breaks loose."

As if on cue, the sky to the north was now a roiling wall of sand and fragments of trees. MacCaully needed to make a decision quickly. She had two choices: retreat to the relative safety of the train station and hope Grady and Rama found shelter of their own, or brave the storm to save her brother. MacCaully cared deeply for Rama and didn't want to see him hurt by her brother. She thought her brother and Philomena were alike in some respects: they went their own ways, mostly alone, and made no apologies for it. But she worried about the kind of life her brother might be stuck with if he didn't stop being so angry, resentful, and destructive. Then Mac-Caully had an epiphany—a moment of certain clarity—about how to proceed. MacCaully and Philomena were cut from the same cloth, both having parents who loved them but were not always around when needed. Mac-Caully was used to making big decisions by herself, just like Philomena. She drew on their connection and had a vision of Philomena pointing directly to Cerro Colorado.

MacCaully shouted to Wyler, "Take me up there now!"

Wyler looked into MacCaully's fierce eyes, pulled her onto Loco, and then they were off.

"There's only one place they can be going, and they better get there fast," said MacCaully.

"Loco! Faster, girl. We gotta cover some ground!" Wyler commanded.

Focusing now on Grady and Rama, Wyler saw them turn to the left about three-quarters of the way up the mountain. "They're going to the old turquoise mine!" he shouted over the din.

MacCaully was spellbound by the rapidly approaching wall of sand and the high-pitched sound of trees snapping. She could hear Loco breathing like a freight train as she struggled to climb the loose, gravelly rock. The cloud

now enveloped the entire village of Lamy. It was as if they were looking down at an ocean of brown, swirling earth.

"We're getting close now!" shouted Wyler. He turned Loco hard to the left on the narrow trail, and MacCaully almost fell off.

"Y'all right?" Wyler called.

MacCaully held Wyler's waist as tightly as she could and yelled against the roar of the storm, "Okay, I think!" Then turning her head, she looked down in horror as the massive haboob covering Lamy like a dark blanket started moving up the mountain, chasing them as if it were alive.

# CHAPTER 10

The setting New Mexico sun blazed down on the travelers as they stood on a dusty road. Noshi smiled at Daisy and Philomena, thinking that he had found his family—one related not by blood and lineage but by spirit and love for one another. Then he turned the painting so he could look at it in the fading light, and had a revelation. "When he painted this, I bet Temporani was painting his exit," he said.

"What do you mean?" asked Daisy.

"He could have painted the temple as a way of returning to it. I'll bet he learned long ago what we've discovered as Imagination Warriors—that the focused power of imagination is transcendent and those with this gift have the ability to traverse time and space instantly," replied Noshi.

Looking at Noshi, Daisy was shocked to see that he
had tucked the painting under his arm and his side had
begun to glow intensely. "Something's happening to the
painting," she said. The golden rays started to pulse
faintly then quickly increased in intensity as they blazed
forth from the painting.

In a panic, Noshi held the painting to his chest, hoping to smother the light, but it kept growing and spreading, making his chest look like a miniature sun.

Philomena opened the doors to the hotel and said,
"Hurry, or we'll attract attention."

With her heart pounding, Daisy glanced at Noshi and
saw that he was now completely enveloped in the eerie
golden light. "Does it hurt?" she asked in a frightened
voice.

"Not at all. Actually it feels pleasant, not scary—like
I'm taking a bath in benevolent light," Noshi replied.

Philomena noticed that Noshi was starting to get a
far-off look.

"I know this painting is just a study," Noshi continued. "I'm willing to bet that Temporani also painted
it small because he planned to travel with it and in
it. For some reason, we don't know why, Temporani
ran into the El Ortiz Hotel, leaving this painting in
the general store. I think he wanted to come back
for it but something prevented him from getting
back. So we should probably try to use this painting
to return to Santa Fe, its original location. If we're
lucky, we'll arrive in our own time in the place we
want to be."

"I didn't want to say it, but I got a really ominous feeling about that big painting of the rock that's hanging in the hallway," said Daisy.

"I'm for jumping into this one," Philomena added.

Noshi started to rub his temples again, indicating that he was in deep thought. "I've been marinating a theory," he finally said, cryptically. "This Mr. Temporani fascinates me. I believe he is the key to all of this. Furthermore, I'm certain that he is the creator of all the other paintings we transited, with the exception of my painting of the Native princess."

Daisy was amused that Noshi was talking like a lawyer building his case in front of a jury.

Noshi continued, "We have become enmeshed in a system of portals connected by paintings. These paintings are unbound by time and space and are, in fact, 'alive.' Imagination Warriors always rejoice in the knowledge that imagination has immense power to transform and illuminate our world, and probably any other world."

"Is there a point to all this or can we get on with our journey now?" said Philomena, tapping her foot.

Noshi ignored Philomena's comment and continued, "Question: what do we have in common with our Mr. Temporani? Answers, anyone?"

Daisy had been formulating her own theory and said, slowly and deliberately, "Noshi's painting of the princess has one important element in common with Mr. Temporani's painting of the temple, and I'll bet with the painting in the Pink Garter Saloon as well."

"Of course, Daisy!" Noshi blurted out. "Why did I not see this before?"

"Perhaps you were just so close to your own painting that you could not see the forest for the trees," Daisy replied.

Beside himself with excitement, Noshi urged, "Daisy, please continue."

"In addition to being conduits of our impressive imaginations, all the paintings have a common denominator: the golden yellow rays radiating outward. Taking the example of Noshi's painting first, the golden rays alerted us that the painting was changing without apparent input from the artist," said Daisy.

"Come to think of it, the painting in the Pink Garter Saloon had golden light peeking out from under the stormy clouds on the horizon!" Philomena pointed out.

"Now we have yet another example—a sketch of a Scottish Rite Temple—that is changing and, I think, telling us to enter it," concluded Daisy.

"I had no idea you were so analytical, Daisy!" Philomena exclaimed.

"You get the merit badge for Imagination Warrior thinking, Daisy," Noshi stated proudly.

"About that yellow paint——" Noshi again massaged his temples then continued: "I bought that paint from an art supply store I'd never been to before. I was walking down Camino Sendero and suddenly saw a tiny art shop I'd never noticed, even though I'd walked that block many times. I went in, and it was like going back in time. Everything—the paints, the brushes, the canvases—looked and smelled really old. I spotted a rack of oil paints displayed on an old easel and gravitated toward a tube of yellow paint. The elderly proprietor claimed it was from the Old Country. So I asked, which old country. 'Italy, of course,' he said, sounding a little offended. He held the yellow paint in his hands like it was a precious commodity and proudly stated, 'I've sourced this paint from an old family supplier in Naples.' Then, with a cryptic wink, he whispered, 'This is what you want.' At the time, I didn't think much about his odd manner of salesmanship, but now I see that it adds to our mystery."

"What a slog that was," Grady muttered under his breath as he and Rama finally entered the mine. He slapped his shirt and pants repeatedly and ran his fingers vigorously through his dark hair to remove all the embedded dirt from the haboob. Rama stared at him stoically.

"Found this hideout by accident a few years ago while scouting for a tucked-away place that I could call my own," Grady said in the direction of Rama.

"What am I carrying, and why is it important to you, Grady?" asked Rama.

Grady looked at Rama for a long time, wondering if he could trust him with his secret. He began to untie the ropes that held the painting to Rama's back.

After the load was removed, Rama took a deep breath and watched as Grady, with some difficulty, placed the object on the dirt floor of the mine. Outside, the sandstorm was still raging. Rama had never experienced a haboob before firsthand, though he had heard of them. He felt strongly that a phenomenon of this magnitude signaled change and tumultuous times ahead since he knew all too well that throughout time strong, destructive winds generally foretold upheaval. He shuddered  at the possibility.

Rama was well read and had traveled widely before he'd been sold to his present family. He had a rich inner life and was aware that he had lived many lives, not all of them as an animal. When he dreamed, he recalled several lives as a human warrior and fearless leader and that he'd sacrificed his life and his men's lives for unworthy and cavalier causes. He was certain that this present life was penance for previous lives of arrogance and violence. He knew Grady was a young soul; the boy's behavior reflected a lack of experience in accumulated lives led on earth. Rama acknowledged the irony of his current situation: this boy with minimal experience had been placed in a position of authority over him. Still, Rama vowed to learn all the lessons necessary to evolve and transcend his station in this life, even if it meant cooperating with Grady to a point.

Grady removed the tarp from the painting and tied its ends to rock outcroppings around the entrance to the cave, hoping to protect them from the blowing sand. Rama saw that the object it had covered was a painting. Now he watched Grady carefully brush debris from its surface, fascinated because he'd never seen Grady be so fastidious with anything.

With the storm fully upon them now, the light began fading from the entrance. Grady held a small flashlight as he carefully wiped the last bit of debris from the painting. The flashlight spotlit the painting in an eerie way, making it seem as though it was the only object in the world. Rama moved closer to the painting, sensing that it was an object of obsession for Grady.

Grady said, almost in a whisper, "I've seen it change before, and now it's changed again. There used to be a third teepee; also, now there are two figures in front of one of the teepees that weren't there before. The smaller figure looks like a girl holding a cat."

Rama leaned in closer and noticed a tiny marking in the lower right corner of the painting that appeared to be a symbol with a signature underneath it. The symbol looked strangely familiar. "I know this symbol, but it's been altered," Rama said.

"What do you mean?" asked Grady.

Rama looked at Grady, trying to judge his mood, then said, "This is the sign for the Freemasons. They were a guild of European stonemasons, dating back many centuries, who knew how to build structures and shared their knowledge with one another, so it was never lost." Grady moved his finger over the symbol as if to emphasize what Rama was explaining to him.

"See the surveyor's compass on top pointing down? Usually, there is a metal right-angle tool with the tip pointing down beneath it, but instead there is what looks like two sun rays at right angles radiating up," added Rama.

"So you think one of those Freemason guys did this picture?" asked Grady.

"They were builders, not painters; but the symbol here is very similar. The Freemason symbol would have had an eye in the center of the surveyor's compass, but in this painting there is a keyhole shape," Rama observed.

Grady wondered what this could mean in connection with the painting's changes or Philomena's interest in it.

Wyler was desperate to find the mine opening. He sensed that they were near it; but the storm had so completely enveloped them that they were unable to get their bearings. MacCaully held Wyler so tightly he could hardly breathe, and pressed her head deep into his back to protect her eyes from the piñon branches that flew about like daggers, whipping them mercilessly.

Remembering that the mine entrance had a concrete base, Wyler looked for something smooth underfoot. Suddenly, Loco tumbled forward in the darkness, pitching Wyler and MacCaully over her mane to the ground.

Wyler reached out in the dark to locate MacCaully. "You okay, Mac?" he shouted.

"I'm dazed but all right!" MacCaully shouted back.

MacCaully touched Loco's front right leg, which was warm and sticky with blood. "Wyler! Loco's hurt!" MacCaully cried. Then she felt Wyler's hand on her shoulder, and he slid beside her.

"I'm sorry, compadre," Wyler said, examining Loco's leg. "I shoulda known to go even slower in this pea soup."

Loco had a deep cut on her leg from a jagged rock at the edge of the trail. Wyler made sure that the leg was not broken. "No break, girl," he uttered, trying to sound optimistic.

MacCaully could see that Wyler and Loco had a special relationship, and she wondered if Loco ever talked to Wyler. She always felt special when Rama talked to her. But when she looked into Loco's eyes she knew Loco didn't have the gift of speech that Rama had, and she felt sad for her.

Wyler removed his red bandana and wrapped it tightly around Loco's bloody leg. "MacCaully, hold my hand," Wyler said as he felt around for the concrete platform. "It's gotta be close," he said, gritting his teeth.

Knowing Wyler was worried about his horse, MacCaully shouted at the top of her lungs, "Grady! Grady, where are you?"

Grady's flashlight was still spotlighting the little figures in the painting. "Sure looks like her and that New York cat," he thought to himself. "But how could that be? And if she can enter a painting, why can't I do it, too? Boy, that would really surprise her!"

Rama became aware of a different sound above the howl of the storm. He moved to the entrance of the mine and pushed the tarp back with his nose. The sky was finally beginning to lighten a little, as if a black veil was being lifted. He heard the sound again and knew it was MacCaully! Rama cried out to her.

An exhausted MacCaully, followed by Wyler walking with a limping Loco, staggered toward Rama. MacCaully used the last bit of her energy to lean into her llama and say, gratefully, "We just knew you had to be close."

Grady turned to the commotion at the front of the mine entrance. He reluctantly pulled himself away from the painting and stood it up against the mine wall, with the back of the painting facing away from the others.

"Why did you follow me?" he asked in a surly voice.

"We nearly got killed out there trying to come help you," MacCaully responded, angrily.

"I didn't ask you to follow me," he countered.

Wyler had a chance to look at Loco's wound in the relative safety of the mine. "It's very close to an artery, compadre," he said, looking up at his friend. Wyler stripped his shirt off, rolled it up, and wrapped it tightly around Loco's damaged leg. Then with a sense of urgency, he peeled the tarp back from the entrance and decided that the storm had lifted enough to descend the mountain. "Mac, Grady, I need to get Loco back down to see a vet right now. She can't afford to lose much more blood. Do you plan to hole up here a while?" he asked.

MacCaully looked to Grady for an answer. "I think we'll wait till the storm completely clears out," Grady said.

"Okay. You can get Mac back down on Rama. But be sure to leave as soon as the storm has cleared. You don't want to be stuck out here after nightfall."

"We will," Grady said.

MacCaully watched as Wyler and Loco hobbled out of the mine into the storm's aftermath, then she turned toward her brother and, pointing to the painting, said, "Is that what you had Rama haul up here? It sure doesn't look like a table."

Grady begrudgingly turned the painting around for his sister to see.

"Hey, that's the painting from the Pink Garter Saloon!" MacCaully exclaimed.

"Good call, Sherlock. I've become an art lover, and I couldn't live without it!" he stated sarcastically.

"Seriously, why did you take it out of the saloon?" MacCaully demanded. "That's stealing."

Grady chose not to answer his sister's question.

Rama was circling closer in on this interesting conversation between siblings. He moved very close to the painting, which reminded him of the work of the German-American artist Albert Bierstadt. "Dear, could you please adjust my glasses? They keep slipping off my nose," he said to MacCaully.

She gently pushed Rama's large, heavy glasses back onto the bridge of his lengthy nose and tightened the rope they were attached to securely around his furry neck. She knew Rama's eyes were weak and gratefully remembered the times when everyone was asleep in her house, Rama had spent hours helping her with homework, and she, in return, had fashioned a crude pair of reading glasses attached to a heavy rope, aware that he loved to read when he was not working—that reading was his sanctuary from the burden of being a pack animal. She had dutifully turned the pages of books for hours as Rama became transported to more wondrous realities.

"This painting is quite beautiful. It seems to ask questions of the viewer. For example, what is the Native American warrior looking at? He appears wary. And what about these tiny figures in the distance? They seem to be fleeing from the teepees," Rama observed.

Wanting to change the subject, Grady said, "I don't know about you, Mac, but I'm staying here in the mine tonight. You can take Rama back home. Looks like the storm's died down now."

MacCaully glanced at Rama for guidance. Rama slowly nodded his big head as if to say, "Let's stay here over-night. It's the wiser thing to do."

"If you're staying, I'm staying," MacCaully said, planting her feet firmly on the ground and crossing her arms. Grady looked at his sister as she glowered at him. He knew that when MacCaully got like this there was no changing her mind.

"Fine," Grady agreed.

The sky grew dark, and they could hear a pack of coyotes howling somewhere in the distance. Grady pulled down the tarp from the mine entrance and offered it to his sister to sleep on. MacCaully thought her brother looked really tired and troubled.

Grady tucked himself into a corner and set the painting against the mine wall next to him. Within minutes, he fell into a deep sleep.

MacCaully sat on the tarp, staring at the painting. "Rama, tell me more of what you know about this picture," she said.

Rama's big, soulful brown eyes absorbed the work of art. He rarely got a chance to enjoy things of beauty. His eyes teared up, and he said, "The painting has a dynamic tension. The Native American man seems to be protecting the people fleeing from the teepees, as if he were a guardian charged with their safety. The grass and the stormy sky are rendered in a way that suggests a coming storm. It's as if the painter is saying, 'A big, important change is coming.'" After a time, Rama continued. "I love this painting. Look here, where the grass on the horizon meets the surprisingly vivid yellow of the setting sun and how the artist is saying, 'Even though times are difficult and the weather is stormy, I will give you hope on the horizon that a better day is coming.' I could live in this work of art. My imagination is the engine for my internal freedom. While I cannot break free from the structures of my life right now, the weight I carry, and the chores I do, I can choose also to live in other worlds through use of my imagination. I know that is why you help me read all those books. They carry me away to places unshackled and free."

MacCaully gave Rama a soulful hug. In that moment, MacCaully felt like Rama was more a parent to her than her own parents. Even at her tender age she knew her llama was imparting lessons that would last a lifetime.

"I want to see that signature and symbol again," Rama requested, kneeling down to look closely at the painting.

With some effort, MacCaully carefully pivoted the painting in the dirt to face Rama. He bowed his head and tried to focus through his glasses. Suddenly, Rama's eyeglasses fell from his nose and landed in the dirt next to the painting.

MacCaully picked them up, brushed the dirt off the lenses, then said, "Oh no, your glasses are broken, Rama!"

Rama was about to comfort MacCaully about his broken glasses when he sensed movement in the painting. "Amazingly, this painting is changing," he said. Rama felt warm wind and rain tickle his ears.

MacCaully could not believe her eyes. The grasses in the center of the painting were swaying in anticipation of the coming storm.

Rama sensed that there must be a sanctuary just on the other side of this painting, and he thanked his power of imagination for delivering him to this place. He thought to himself, "I would leap at the chance to enter a different reality from the one the fates have decreed for me in this lifetime." Rama then began chanting softly, "I want to be delivered, I want to be delivered from this world."

As MacCaully's eyes were drawn more into the painting, she had the strangest thought. "That girl in the painting looks like Philomena, and that cat looks like Daisy. But why would they be in this painting? Come to think of it, I haven't seen them around lately."

Rama kept his large, brown eyes closed, afraid that if he opened them he would be back in his old reality, a beast of burden in an abandoned turquoise mine atop a

mountain in the high desert of New Mexico. Instead, he imagined the gentle, warm rain falling, heard the hypnotic swaying of the tall grasses, and felt the caressing winds of a gathering summer storm.

And then everything changed. MacCaully and Rama were thrust through some kind of threshold as they tumbled into the painting. It was dark. MacCaully was terrified and held Rama tightly. Rama finally opened his eyes and was confronted with nothingness—no sounds, no light, no movement. And then everything changed again. Rama said reassuringly to MacCaully, "I don't feel we need to be afraid. I think we're on a journey somewhere, even though I don't see us moving. Stay close to me, dear one."

They began to hear sounds—murmurs, laughter, crying — increasing and decreasing in volume but always barely audible, like people at a party talking in another room.

Rama felt a sensation he had not experienced in many years—relief. He was unburdened for the first time in his llama life. All he could think about in that moment were the numerous book pages MacCaully had so patiently turned for him. All the ideas, worlds, and flights of imagination he had experienced while reading had culminated in this moment of deliverance.

# CHAPTER 11

The early morning light filtered through the little window of the tiny, cloistered stone room on the third story of the long-abandoned and forgotten wing of the Scottish Rite Temple in Santa Fe and fell upon Mr. Temporani's weathered, sun-damaged hand as it moved slowly and deliberately across the surface of some old parchment paper. The ruddy-red charcoal stick was a blunt instrument for rendering a study, but he chose it purposely for its ability to depict quickly and expressively whatever he imagined. He would make a larger painting of this study in time. He appeared to be a frail, small man in his seventies with short white hair and a delicate, chiseled nose, but an astute observer would sense something extraordinary about him. Mr. Temporani slowly removed his ancient reading glasses and deliberately placed them on the drawing table. He squinted through weary gray eyes and reflected on his long life of many centuries, thinking, "How many sunrises have I witnessed, how many paintings completed, how many experiences tucked away in the vault of memories? Far too many. One human being cannot be asked to remember the myriad memories accumulated over the centuries—the wars, disasters, endless tragedies, and friendships that by design were destined for failure."

Then he closed his tired eyes and recalled a singular memory that the ravages of time had not erased. Slowly looking down at his hands, through a kind of sense memory he recalled the first time he had come in contact with the special yellow pigment. He smiled, thinking about its ancient Italian name: Giallo di Napoli. His first sight of the brilliant yellow pigment had been like witnessing a miniature sun glow with vibrant color. He had been a much younger man then, full of ambition and arrogance, trying to make his way in the world of art. He had sought out clients who might commission works that he'd gladly paint, eventually finding a theater company that needed a large but unwieldy mural created for a stage play about the powers of the heavens. It was his very first commission, and he was determined to get it exactly right. He'd worked well into the night painting the enormous mural, having to complete it outdoors because it was so large.

Even at his advanced age, he could recall the mysterious quarry in Naples Italy, from which the yellow pigment had been mined. He'd asked the guild of stonemasons that owned the quarry, and used the beautiful marble mined there in the construction of its building projects, for permission to enter the site. As he had stood at the edge of the deep quarry in Naples and peered down into the bowels of the earth, something had caught his artist's eye and he'd asked the foreman if he could descend to the bottom. He had been seeking new pigments to use in his paintings, and in the veins of the earth he had found a prize, an exquisite yellow color. With a shovel and the strength of a young man's back, he had dug out the pigment and, with a satisfied smile, had packed his spoils into one of his only possessions, a leather backpack; hoisted it on his back; and climbed out of the quarry.

Upon his return home, with great anticipation he had emptied the contents of his pack on his dining table as the sun was setting. To his great surprise, the pigment lying on the modest table glowed in the fading light as if pulsating with energy. With curiosity, he had immediately crushed some of the pigment in his granite mortar and pestle and applied it to a simple study already under-way. "This color is perfect for the brilliance of the sun bathing the church in light," he had thought to himself. He did not know it in that moment, but his life would, as a result, be irrevocably changed.

In the wee hours of the morning, after he had finally stopped painting, satisfied that he'd captured an exqui-site new method of rendering sunlight, he had sat back and admired the results. "A good night's work this is," he had told himself. By the time the light of early morning had crept into his modest studio, he was so transfixed by the painting's brilliant yellow luminosity that he felt as if he were having an out-of-body experience. Rendered almost breathless by the intense, deep lapis lazuli blue of the heavens at their zenith, he recalled a perplexing choice he'd made when, after penciling in the figure of a young woman suspended in space above the church, he'd decided to paint over her with the magnificent shade of blue. The enchanting warmth of the sunlight radiating from the walls of the ancient church had convinced him that this first attempt would eventually become a finished work with something indescribably magical about it.

Soon after, he had returned enthusiastically to the immense commissioned mural, excited that his precious yellow pigment would find a suitable home somewhere on the giant canvas. Upon later delivering the completed mural to his client, he had thought, "What a fitting subject matter for my first commissioned work: a constellation of twelve luminous stars against a deep blue vaulting sky set above a calm ocean with just the faintest ripples playing on its surface." He recalled that the theater company commissioning the work had made a last-minute request for him to paint twelve corresponding high-backed regal chairs set in the ocean beneath the celestial array. How he had reveled in the challenge of depicting such a heavenly themed mural!

The young artist's first journey had begun, and with it an inner sense of unfathomable powers. From that moment on, he had understood that the special yellow pigment, in conjunction with his imagination, was an alchemical combination enabling him to traverse time and space at will. He also knew that any transit taken required that he bring a small amount of the paint with him to use for returning home. Consequently, from time to time he had gone back to the quarry to gather more yellow pigment from the bottom of the dig site for future use.

Temporani looked around his simple, spare room. The sole purpose of his living space was to further his pursuit of art and ongoing explorations through time and space. That arcane and ancient yellow pigment, applied imaginatively on canvas, was his vehicle for transiting time and space. On days of weakness and introspection, he felt cursed to have lived so long, to know that loss was a traveler always following him. Over the many centuries, he had witnessed the dangerous stupidity of his fellow humans and thus often experienced sadness, death, conflict, and corruption, only rarely alleviated by the few elevated souls who enriched the world with their presence. As a result, he had begun to limit his engagement with people and, though it had taken centuries, had become isolated and insulated from the tumult of humankind. Now he was content to live in his little stone temple with his art, his memories, his transcendent imagination, and his ability to transit into and out of what he called "the *continuo*," otherwise known as the continuum.

Surveying his tiny, cloistered sanctuary, he thought to himself, "Not many material possessions to show for a five-hundred-year-old man, but evidence of a wealth of adventures riding the imagination." His few possessions were things he could not live without: his backpack, reading glasses, several gold coins sewn into his brown traveling blazer, his trusty fedora, and an old artist's curiosity that had never been quenched throughout all his centuries of travel. Perhaps his most important item was his weathered, leather backpack, tailor-made in Italy long ago. Its sole purpose was safe transport for his brushes, rolled canvases, paints, and his special yellow pigment. He had long before intuited that a simple, monastic life of travel, freedom, observation, and artistic imagination was his destiny. He just hadn't counted on it lasting so long.

Temporani walked over to the backpack. Before transiting, it was his routine to confirm that it held enough Giallo di Napoli in a glass jar, and to make sure the top was securely fastened; his life would depend on it. Once a transit was complete, he would take a visual inventory of his immediate surroundings. His survival skills were finely tuned as he had relied on them for centuries.

Temporani had been drawn to Santa Fe in the early 1900s along with other artists of the time. He had painted a spare desert landscape with tall, jagged mountains rising high from the sweltering desert floor, his characteristic golden Naples sun rays radiating skyward behind the mountain. He had always maintained that there was something indescribable about the high desert light, something pure and distilled, as though it had been created by a deity. "How strange," he thought. "I have been to some of the most exotic and celebrated places on earth, and yet this barren desert location holds me spellbound."

Over the many centuries, he had compared the relative qualities of light in the places to which he had traveled, finding that the clarity and sharpness of New Mexico's light was strangely similar to the light of Venice, Italy. Painting that quality of desert light had always been a joyous, liberating experience. Temporani felt that Santa Fe and Venice shared a special kinship of illumination and spirit. Light and its ability to illuminate the substance and contours of life was of endless fascination to him.

It had been necessary for Temporani to move every forty or fifty years. Though he was an inconspicuous man, he had moved on whenever people began to talk about him. He was never comfortable with attention and was concerned that others might discover his secret powers and means of travel through time and space. Over the centuries he had only made one painting with a human figure in it, and that was a Native American warrior. Being alive as long as he had been and having seen so much stupidity, he had an ingrained apprehension about his human brethren. There had been only two people to whom he had entrusted his time-travel secret, due to necessity: Beecham and Nahimana, the Native American warrior.

Temporani became aware that randomness can be as powerful a force as intention when he had encountered the slightly addled train aficionado Beecham in his Pullman car on an abandoned railroad track in the village of Lamy and made a pact with him to store paintings. After creating many paintings, Temporani had realized he needed more storage space than was possible in his little room in the Scottish Rite Temple. Temporani had been drawn to the unassuming village of Lamy due to its location between an arroyo on the east and low-rolling mountains to the west, with train tracks in the middle. Being highly attuned to temporal anomalies, he had chosen the village to be his second base of operation. He had taken a trip to Santa Fe to purchase art supplies, and as his train car pulled into the Lamy station he'd had a familiar feeling of passing over a threshold to a place with temporal anomalies. He had thought to himself, "In that Pullman car behind the cottonwood trees there's a time and space *continuo* present. I wonder if the current owner knows of the mysterious train car's properties? I can sense *infinito*, infiniteness, within it." He had always known that artists were opportunists at heart and had decided there might be an opportunity to store more of his vast inventory of paintings in the train, where no one would suspect their existence. Subsequently, he had introduced himself to the train car's owner, Beecham, with whom he made an agreement.

Temporani smiled as he recalled first meeting the Native American warrior Nahimana, the other man in whom he had confided. Though separated by age, culture, and language, they had developed deep respect for each other and come to an agreement about storing Temporani's paintings out of sight.

After making sure his backpack was ready for travel, Temporani ambled to the center of his stone sanctuary. There, backlit in the morning sun, was a reworking of a painting he'd completed years before—an image depicting his next destination, one he'd already visited. He took a deep breath, knowing there was a sizable debt to pay and determined to pay it.

Temporani preceded every transit with contemplation and focused concentration, something at which he was adept, given his chosen life of solitude and stillness. He stood in front of a painting, as he had done for half a millennium, and surrendered to his arcane, ancient practice, allowing his imagination to carry him away. Soon his stone sanctuary became suffused with the familiar golden light as the painting morphed and stretched. As a young man experiencing his first transits from painting to painting, he'd almost been overwhelmed by sensory experiences of darkness, light, sounds, voices, wind, and a flashing star field, but now his transits, while still extraordinary adventures, were less challenging.

In all his thousands of portal transits, he'd never seen another soul. However, on rare occasions he thought he had seen figures walking the spectral bridges that seemed to span the void of the infinite time-space continuum, forming pathways and doorways. He had considered the possibility of encountering another soul in transit and wondered how he would react. He had thought to himself, "Am I unique in the world, or are there others like me? If I were to meet fellow travelers in the *continuo*, what would be my reaction? What would I say, and how would I feel? Would those others on a similar path wish to harm me or would they embrace a fellow traveler in the void?" Such possibilities had seemed potentially threatening since part of Temporani's makeup was an ingrained distrust of fellow human beings and a desire to be left alone to create and live in peace.

As Philomena, Noshi, and Daisy huddled in the dark corridor adjoining the great room of the El Ortiz Hotel, they heard comforting sounds of muffled conversations from the hotel's lobby. An almost garish golden light was now emanating from the keyhole of Temporani's little painting of the Scottish Rite Temple. Noshi propped the painting against the wall under the enormous painting of the red rock. "Fellow Imagination Warriors, let us focus our attention and imagination on this work of art," he said.

Daisy began to imagine walking up the steep steps that led to the keyhole-shaped doorway now bathed in the warm, healing golden light. Noshi imagined the yellow light traveling outward into space and continuing endlessly into the ether. Philomena imagined something more earthbound, a vision of her parents standing in front of her and of running toward them, culminating in a loving embrace.

Daisy then gently pawed the corner of the painting where the stairway began and led up to the keyhole-shaped doorway.

"Hey why are you touching the painting, Daisy?" asked Philomena.

Daisy was having a revelation and replied, "I don't think Temporani knew what to do with this painting. Logically, you'd think he'd use it to time travel, but it's unfinished and I doubt he ever used it that way. I think it had powers that terrified him because he didn't understand how to control them. Remember when the golden rays coming out of the Native American princess's crown of feathers in Noshi's painting spread upward? You didn't paint that, Noshi; some other force did. I think this study and your painting have that force in common. But in the case of Temporani's work he may have had no clue how to harness its powers."

The yellow light of the painting was now filling the entire corridor and beginning to spill into the main hallway. For the first time, Noshi noticed something in the painting he'd not seen before. "Look above the temple, way up at the top of the painting—those twelve faint stars."

Daisy's fur tingled with anticipation of another revelation. She now gently pressed both paws on the canvas, slowly moving them as though walking the steps and sensing what it would feel like to enter the temple and be immersed in its golden light. "I feel that the painting is encoded with instructions somehow," she said.

Noshi drew closer, touching the uppermost part of the canvas, where the arc of faint stars was painted.

Daisy's fur now tingled so intensely it was like an electric current running through her body. She said, "I'm sensing that those without the gift consider this a throwaway study, but there is so much information buried in it. I sense that the stars are foretelling an important gathering." Daisy closed her eyes and concentrated, then continued, adding, "The stars represent twelve beings who will convene here in the temple."

"Do you mean people like us?" asked Philomena.

Noshi chimed in, saying, "We might be the guests of honor!"

Daisy appeared to be going into a trance and, swaying slowly, said, "Beings like us, yes, but there are others as well who are not human. Temporani's yellow paint is the key here. It's unique and the reason we must take the painting with us."

Noshi heard voices getting louder in the hallway. The painting's light had spilled into the outer corridor and was calling unwanted attention to the three travelers. "We must hurry slowly, Imagination Warriors. Touch the canvas, and in your imaginations 'see' us taking it with us into the continuum," he said with urgency.

Anyone turning the corner of the hallway at that instant would have witnessed a very curious sight—Philomena and Noshi kneeling next to the painting and Daisy at eye level with it, all bathed in glowing light, touching Temporani's painting and then disappearing into a wall of radiant golden light. The three travelers felt the now-familiar sensation of traveling at high speed in the darkness.

Immediately, Noshi looked for the painting and sighed with relief when he saw it safely tucked under his arm. Philomena and Daisy noticed something different about the painting, however. "The keyhole-shaped doorway's light is dim again, the way it was when we first noticed the painting beginning to change," Daisy observed.

"The painting must have used a lot of power making the jump with us," ruminated Philomena.

"Next up, the wind, please!" said Philomena.

As if on cue, the familiar warm, humid air began to move all around them. Noshi was mindful to hold the little painting securely as the wind increased in intensity. Daisy fondly remembered when she was a kitten and Mrs. Z had taken her for a bicycle ride in Central Park; she had closed her eyes and experienced a delicious sensation of wind in her face as the bike moved forward. She then glanced at Noshi's little painting and had the strangest feeling that it was linked to them by imagination.

Noshi looked ahead and behind him as though he'd lost something. "Noshi, what is it?" Philomena asked.

"It almost seems too calm right now," he said apprehensively. As they saw the ghostly spectral bridge and spidery filaments stretch out in front of them in the void, Noshi felt the painting under his arm resist his hold on it, as if a powerful gyroscope within it was fighting for balance. Noshi slowly eased his grip on the painting without letting go of it.

"What's happening?" asked Philomena.

"Not sure. The painting seems to want to face forward," Noshi said.

"What if you let it do what it wants to do?" said Daisy.

Noshi took her advice, and the painting started moving on its own into the void, sending a pulse of light out through the keyhole-shaped doorway.

"It's as though it is directing us to something out there," Daisy reasoned.

The painting's light ray beamed out in front of them like a beacon in the night, searching for something. Daisy's fur began to tingle. "Look, the beam is catching something up ahead that's moving fast, as though it wants us to see it," she said excitedly.

Noshi stared into the void and tried to make sense of what they were all seeing. The beam of light blasting from the painting illuminated what looked like a human figure about two hundred feet above them, moving toward them at a high rate of speed. Daisy was first to feel the shockwave that preceded the object. Whatever was in front was being violently pushed aside like a fast-moving boat through water, and the wave was rocking the three travelers on their spectral bridge. Daisy noted that the color and shape of the wake, however, made it look nothing like any boat wake she had ever seen. The figure behind the wake looked like a small man wearing a hat and carrying something big on his back, but the wave was distorting the image of the figure, stretching it vertically and horizontally.

"It's like a kaleidoscopic bullet shell moving through the transit! I wonder if we look like that to him?" murmured Noshi.

A shiver ran through Daisy as Noshi said that.

The kaleidoscopic bullet shell raced past them at great speed. Daisy wasn't sure, but she thought she saw a little man with a hat and backpack looking at them, surprised as he sped by. "That's Temporani! I just know it!" shouted Daisy with certainty.

"Where is he going, and are we going where he came from?" asked Noshi.

"Does he know we have his painting?" asked Philomena.

"Bet he does now," said Daisy said in a sassy voice.

Temporani had only a few seconds to process what was happening below him. For the first time in all his travels through the *continuo* he saw others on the spectral bridges, which terrified him. He struggled to understand the implications of what he had seen, thinking it seemed like three figures, a man, a child, and perhaps a small animal. A frame held some sort of painting glowing with light. "Why? Were they artists, too?" he asked himself. "But the painting looked familiar. They must have seen me as well. Their trajectory appeared to be directed toward where I came from. Are they going to the temple? What do they know?" A chill ran through his old body as he had a realization: "They must have my painting of the temple. The beacon light is unmistakable. I wonder if they know about its power. Oh God, they're going to the temple!" He cursed himself when he remembered that he'd left the painting at the general store. "I've been on too many transits over too many years. I'm a senile old fool," he thought.

Though Temporani had created the painting, he could hardly take credit for what it had become. Subconsciously, he realized he might have left it for others to discover, as he had found its power confounding. Unlike the other paintings he'd done using the magical Giallo de Napoli pigment to time travel, this one seemed cursed, as though the gift of time travel that once freed him from humanity's follies had now turned against him in dark and mysterious ways. It seemed to hold a power over him, suggesting things about the future that he didn't understand; demanding his attention by pulsing

light when he ignored it; and changing in ways he could not comprehend. He remembered when the twelve stars he had not painted appeared above the temple, and the yellow rays of light began pulsing as if attempting to communicate important things to him. Even though he had used his extraordinary yellow pigment to paint light emanating from the temple's keyhole-shaped entrance, he knew deep down that the beam of light functioned as a beacon to contact others who might understand its meaning, though he could not fathom its purpose. "Did the travelers on the spectral bridge understand its power? Had they solved the riddle of the stars?" He wondered anxiously about these ominous developments.

Rama opened his eyes. He sensed that he and MacCaully were moving somewhere. The warm wind rushing around them felt pleasurable, even though it occurred in absolute darkness. MacCaully was terrified at the thought that she had fallen into a dark void with no chance of escape. She held on tightly to her llama.

Rama's sensitive ears felt the warm, humid wind moving faster. He wanted to protect MacCaully. She was young and frightened and really needed his strength right now. "Stay close to me, and we will remain safe," he said. Rama recalled lives spent as a father and was always protective of MacCaully as she was so much like a daughter to him.

Rama now heard sounds and saw images that he interpreted as glimpses into his past lives—sounds of someone speaking in Spanish and images of a desert and battle, swords clashing and firearms being discharged, and powerful war horses racing, their mounts carrying red flags. He forced himself not to blink for fear he would miss something, even though some of the images were difficult to witness.

"Rama, what is happening to us? I'm scared," Mac-Caully cried.

"Dear child, you know that I will always protect you," Rama said reassuringly. That seemed to calm her down a bit, and then Rama, remembering a sweet child's lullaby he'd sung to her when she was very young, hummed it for her.

Eventually, the black void gave way to an eerie half-light, like the light of a full moon. Rama said enthusiastically to MacCaully, "Look up, the stars are coming out—millions of brilliant stars!"

MacCaully was awed then overwhelmed by the cosmic display. She closed her eyes and hugged Rama tightly.

Even though Daisy felt that she'd answered some of the important questions about the painting and Temporani, there were many more to resolve. She looked at Noshi, who was bathed in the golden light, and saw that the rays reaching out from the center of the keyhole-shaped door-way illuminated an intricate network of other spectral bridges, some faint or incomplete, as though lacking a clear destination.

Noshi struggled to gain control of the painting. "I feel resistance from the painting if I point it in any direction in which it doesn't want to go," he explained.

"In what direction do the rays want to go?" asked Daisy.

Noshi pointed the painting straight up, and the beams seemed to lock onto coordinates in the void above them, as though preprogrammed.

Their motion on the spectral bridge had slowed, and the warm wind had ceased. Daisy and Philomena both looked at Noshi, who was holding the painting as if it were a compass, finding true north. All three looked up to see more spectral bridges become visible, illuminated by the beam of light.

Suddenly, a rush of air thrust them upward, where they rode the beams of light emanating from the temple painting. Daisy felt as though she was riding an incredibly fast elevator straight up to the hundredth floor of a skyscraper.

Then they experienced the characteristic sights and sounds of entering a new reality—first the faint sounds of voices and then the stroboscopic light, as though they were moving at great speed through an underground tunnel with overhead lamps. After a while, Daisy tumbled onto a cold, hard floor. Philomena followed through the portal and almost landed on her companion. Noshi had the presence of mind to protect the painting as he, too, fell hard on the floor.

Disoriented and a little cranky from multiple portal transits, the three travelers saw they were in a small room with a cold, stone floor. The very first thing Daisy noticed was the smell. "This place smells old to me," she said, wrinkling her little nose.

Surveying the room slowly, Noshi said, "I feel at home here. I think I know why."

Standing in the middle of the old room was an easel with a painting on it. They moved closer to it and immediately realized they must be in Temporani's studio.

# CHAPTER 12

Rama felt happy and unburdened for the first time in his long llama life. Looking up at the vaulted firmament of brilliant stars—brighter than any stars visible back at home—he felt at peace and one with all around him. MacCaully was apprehensive about their extraordinary circumstances, but she took comfort in knowing that her friend, protector, and part-time father was there to help her. She wanted her llama to know that she was growing up and able to handle this unusual situation so Rama would be proud of her.

Rama moved his big, furry head next to MacCaully's face and looked into her fearful eyes. "Dear child, please trust me. I know that we will be all right."

At that very second, a strong wave of air rocked them on their bridge as what looked like a large, elongated shiny capsule rocketed past them at incredible speed.

"Rama, what was that?" MacCaully pleaded.

Rama thought it had the properties of ice, water, and light all bound up together. He kept his eyes on the object as it became an increasingly tiny point of light in front of them.

MacCaully looked up and asked, "Where are we going, Rama?"

Rama had experienced lots of bizarre and inexplicable things in his many lives, but he chose to communicate the best possible outcome of this extraordinary situation they found themselves in. "I can't be sure, but if I had to hazard a guess I'd say that we've managed to enter the painting and are now traveling through it. Maybe the painting back there was an entry point, like a portal to another place at which we will eventually arrive. And maybe we are not the only ones doing this."

Temporani had to admit that he had been completely unnerved by the experience of seeing other travelers in the *continuo*. His well-honed survival skills made him resolve to move quickly and be cautious upon arriving through the portal. It was still dark outside when he emerged, but, looking at the sky through the opening in the teepee, Temporani could see the fingers of the dawn's light to the east. The warm-colored teepee hides moving slowly in the breeze were comforting to the weary old traveling artist. He took his backpack off and made sure the contents were all there. Suddenly, someone struck him hard on the side of his head. Temporani fell to the dirt floor and instinctively grabbed his backpack, but a young man standing over him wrenched it away.

"What do you want?" Temporani asked.

"I want your backpack, and I want to know where I am," he demanded.

"I'm just an old hiker, and I need my backpack," Temporani said as he realized that he was being confronted by a teenager who was maybe sixteen or seventeen years old.

Temporani watched in horror as the teenager emptied the contents of the leather backpack, including the jar of golden paint, on the ground. His mind was on fire as he considered the consequences of losing his special paint. Without it applied to a painting, he'd never be able to return home, or anywhere else for that matter. It would mean the end of freedom as he knew it. He let out a sigh of relief when the jar did not break on impact.

"We are in North Dakota, on sacred Sioux land," Temporani told the teenager.

"Why are we in a teepee?" the boy barked.

"You have traveled unconventionally. The year is 1833," revealed Temporani.

The boy dropped the backpack and held his hands to his head as if to calm himself down. Temporani noted that he was dressed in black jeans and sneakers and must have come from a future time. The boy took short, shallow breaths, trying to recover from the information he had been given.

"My name is Mr. Temporani. What is your name?" Temporani asked, holding out a hand in welcome.

"Grady," the boy said slowly, reaching out to help Temporani up. "If you're a hiker, why do you have art supplies in your pack?"

"I paint landscapes. I'm waiting for sunrise to begin painting," Temporani replied.

"Painting. I...I think I fell through a painting," Grady sputtered.

"Can you describe the painting?" Temporani asked.

"Sure, it was a western painting of an Indian on a rock, with teepees in the background," Grady offered. As he looked at his surroundings, his jaw slowly dropped in wonder. "I'm actually *in* the painting. That's wild," he concluded.

"Yes," said Temporani, as he surreptitiously gathered his belongings and began returning them to his backpack.

The jar of yellow paint was next to the boy's foot. He reached for it, but Grady picked it up and inquired, "What's in this jar? Is it gold?"

"Just yellow paint," Temporani said innocently as he watched Grady turn the jar around in his hands.

"Where was this painting?" Temporani asked, keeping his eyes fixed on the jar.

Grady watched as the old man dusted himself off, then replied, "I took it from the Pink Garter Saloon in Lamy yesterday."

Temporani's eyes widened. Now he knew the painting was his. "What year is it for you back in Lamy?" Temporani asked as he reached for the jar of paint in Grady's hands.

Grady pulled the jar close to his chest and replied, "It's 2016, but where I live it still looks like 1916."

Temporani needed to somehow get the paint back. He wasn't sure what this boy might do with it, and if it were lost he'd be trapped forever. With his mind racing, he thought to himself, "If the boy takes my paint, he'll potentially hold the key to time travel, and who knows what terrifying consequences would follow. This teenage boy is dangerous in many ways. Make sure he understands that this is normal paint and not worth anything. And make sure you get the jar back in one piece. The rest of the backpack's contents are expendable."

Grady turned to look at the painting resting on the easel, seemingly still confused by its contents. Mr. Temporani knew all too well what it depicted: "El Ortiz Hotel, circa 1930, the Depression era."

Grady moved closer to the painting, turning his back to Temporani. With stealth summoned by the necessity for survival, Temporani stepped up behind him, grabbed the jar from his hands, activated his powers of imagination, and pushed him into the painting. He knew his actions were poorly thought out and would probably haunt him, yet he had to get the paint back. He told himself that he would eventually travel back in time to retrieve the boy but had other commitments to meet first.

Daisy was first to recognize that the painting was a slightly different version of the one of the Native American warrior. "There are only two teepees in the background of this painting, and the sky is placid, looking

like dawn will break any minute now. The painting in the Pink Garter Saloon, however, had a stormy sky with the last rays of light peeking through the clouds at the horizon," she noted.

Noshi thought to himself, "Someone has moved one of the teepees. Why? Were they being threatened in some way? Would Temporani travel back to a picture he'd already painted?" Looking around, he noticed the little bed on the stone floor and the tiny bathroom in the corner. He remarked, "This is unmistakably Temporani's home. Look at all the painting supplies strewn about. This is the dwelling of the man who has painted all these pictures we keep falling into. This person lives simply, like a monk. There is something reverential—almost holy—about this room."

Then all three travelers focused on the one window in the small stone room, noticing it was keyhole shaped, just like the doorway in the painting they'd carried through the portal. Immediately recognizing where they were, Philomena shouted, "It's Santa Fe! I see the old post office across the street and all the adobe buildings!"

"It may be Santa Fe, but when?" Noshi asked. After looking at the cars with their long, straight hoods that seemed like coffins, swoopy fenders, and huge whitewall tires, Noshi concluded, "The 1920s, I think, by the look of the cars."

Philomena's heart sank when she saw how old the cars were, knowing that she was still decades from home, even if they were in nearby Santa Fe.

Daisy looked at Philomena and said reassuringly, "We'll get back to our time and place, and we'll do it together."

Noshi was fascinated with the artist's room. He walked slowly around its perimeter and sensed that time stood still within its confines. "An artist's space says a lot about the artist," Noshi mused. "Here is a man who does not care about material things. He probably just wants to be left alone to paint. Imagination Warriors, it's again time to assess our circumstances. Shall we?"

The three sat in a circle on the stone floor. "We find ourselves back in our home state of New Mexico," said Noshi. "Unfortunately, we've arrived about ninety-six years too early. Apparently, our only exit from this place is the painting we just came through. My assumption is that this painting would send us right back to the teepee landscape we originally entered, and that does not serve us." Noshi pointed to the painting resting on the easel in the center of the room.

Daisy smiled when she realized that Noshi was thoroughly enjoying his role as kind of a game show host.

"Okay," he continued, "here's what we think we know. The man known to us as Temporani has painted all these portal paintings: the one of the Native American warrior crouching on the boulder, the one of El Ortiz Hotel, and the one of the Scottish Rite Temple in which we currently find ourselves. But why would the artist choose to return to one that he's already painted?" Noshi rubbed his hands together and formed a steeple with them.

"We have done what is considered impossible," he continued. "We have moved through portals of time and space created by paintings with the aid of two important elements: imagination and the yellow paint that is common to all the paintings through which we've traveled."

"But what about your painting of the Native princess, the one that started this whole journey? You didn't use Temporani's yellow paint," said Daisy analytically.

Noshi replied, "I've been thinking about that ever since we realized that Temporani's magical paint was the common denominator of the portal paintings except for my painting. Do you remember me telling you about the time I wandered down an old Santa Fe street and happened upon a tiny art supply store I'd never seen before?"

Daisy and Philomena nodded attentively.

"Well, the old proprietor was pushing a particularly obscure brand of paints sourced from Naples, Italy, and mined from a quarry originally owned by Freemasons in the Middle Ages. He said he'd researched that quarry and discovered that in addition to the marble the Freemasons had mined there they had found a unique vein of natural minerals. The store owner also told me that in the Middle Ages if a new paint pigment was found, its location was kept top secret so others wouldn't discover the potentially valuable pigment. These facts might account for the paint Temporani used in his paintings. And I might have used the very same type of pigment to paint the crown of my Native princess since I bought yellow paint from the old man, who wouldn't let me leave without purchasing it. The store owner was apparently a student of the geology of that Naples area, and as I was considering whether or not to buy the yellow paint, which was very expensive, he had said, "*Uranio*. There is uranium in the Giallo de Napoli."

Daisy asked skeptically, "So you think the uranium in the natural minerals accounts for the yellow paint's ability to enable viewers to transcend time and space?"

Noshi replied, "I think it's entirely plausible that an alchemical reaction could occur between the radioactive pigment and the imagination. Do you remember me telling you both that being a true Imagination Warrior means thinking unconventionally? Well, you need look no further than this little room to confirm how the power of imagination has been harnessed in magical ways by the creator of these paintings."

Temporani still was not happy about sending a young man time traveling without his consent, but resolved to deal with the consequences later. He carefully placed all his art supplies in his backpack, grateful not to have lost the Giallo di Napoli, which would have meant the end of his freedom to span the ages and would have marooned him in the place where it had been destroyed or stolen. Freedom and his ability to create were everything to Temporani.

A hazy sun finally rose over the grassy plains, and the old artist hoisted his backpack over his shoulder and walked out into the morning light with a slight limp, resulting from his encounter with the boy. He cast his eyes toward the big boulder up ahead, where his friend would be waiting according to their agreement. He reflected back to the time when he had first created this painting in which he now was walking. "A nomadic soul requires a safe place in which to rest," he thought to himself.

The grasses were swaying slowly, and the air had a hint of sweet water in it. He breathed in the aromatic, humid air and ran his hands through the tall grasses as he walked and reflected. In all his years of travel through time and space, he had never allowed himself to grow close to anyone, always wary of being found out. Nahimana was a stoic sort, not unlike himself. They both liked their own company and being close to the earth. Temporani loved this place out on the Great Plains of North America. He found serenity here; the expansiveness of the big sky was a balm to his soul.

He recalled the first time he had met Nahimana. He'd decided, yet again, that he would need a place to protect portal paintings that he'd created over time, and the vast prairie landscape suited his purposes. He'd traveled by rail and then hiked, carrying his backpack, portable easel, and paints through the prairie lands of North Dakota. Upon cresting a low hill that overlooked a valley of swaying prairie grasses, he had seen the exquisitely sculpted boulder in the foreground, then the three white teepees in the distance that reminded him of ships with white sails cruising tranquilly on the ocean. "How beautiful and perfect this place is," he had thought. Just then a Native American warrior strode from behind the boulder, confident and questioning. "Where is your weapon?" he had asked Temporani in a disarming fashion. "I have no weapon;

I have paints and canvas. Such things are considered weapons to some," Temporani had replied. The warrior had smiled, and a friendship began.

Over the years, Nahimana had overseen the increasing inventory of paintings created by his friend. The completed works of art had been stored in some of the teepees and in underground caves. Nahimana and his tribal brothers and sisters had been willing to assist the strange little man who wore a hat and backpack, and he had even been allowed to engage in their ceremonies and rituals. All they had required as payment for their vigilance had been gold coins.

As if on cue, Nahimana dismounted his horse at the base of the boulder. He was tall and sinewy, his body language reflecting a wariness that he shared with Temporani.

The old traveler relaxed and released the tension he'd been feeling. "My brother, a man of your word always, thank you for your presence," Temporani said quietly.

The Plains warrior looked down kindly at him. "You are hurt?" the warrior inquired, referring to his friend's limp.

Temporani glanced back at the teepee, shook his head, and replied, "Not important, but vigilance is needed."

Nahimana nodded knowingly. "Always, my brother."

"As per our agreement," Temporani said as he held out the gold coins for Nahimana.

"Thank you, my friend," Nahimana replied.

They walked for a while in silence through the tall grasses toward the three teepees in the distance. Then Nahimana said, "There was flooding from a fierce storm, and we moved some paintings from one of the teepees into the cave to protect them. We have evidence that

three travelers entered our camp from the hotel painting and then left quickly, but they did not see us. The
paintings in the other two teepees are intact and safe.
The dark train interior and the hotel great room await."

Temporani's face went white as a sheet. "Were these
travelers the ones I saw on the spectral bridge? Are they
following me, and if so to what end?" he thought to himself.

"You are troubled, my brother. How may I help?"
Nahimana asked his friend.

"I want to enter my train interior painting," explained
Temporani.

Nahimana nodded agreement and replied, "Yes, my
brother, safe travels."

They stood for a moment at the entrance to the teepee. Then Temporani parted the animal hides and looked
at the ominously dark charcoal painting of the train interior, with its characteristic golden light spilling in through
the train's windows.

"We cannot reenter this painting. We'll be caught in an endless loop," cautioned Daisy. They were staring at yet another
version of the painting from the Pink Garter Saloon, this
one also of the Native American warrior and the teepees.

Noshi was in deep thought. "Occultism...mysticism...
secret societies," he mumbled to himself.

"What are you saying?" Philomena asked.

"Got a hunch," he said. He looked out the window to his
left and noticed that there were three other keyhole-shaped

stone windows just like it. The only difference was that their window, which was at the end of the row, appeared to be an old gray-stone color while the rest of the temple building was the characteristic pink color that the Scottish Rite Temple had been since its construction at the turn of the century.

Noshi said, "I have a feeling that this is a forgotten wing of the temple. For whatever reason, it's been unpainted."

"Maybe the artist is safe here because nobody knows that anyone's here," Daisy posited.

"Okay, so what do we do now?" Philomena asked.

Noshi paced around the little room, thinking. "I was here once in the past . . . I mean the future," he said with a smile. "They have tours here by appointment. You have to make a reservation, and one of the Masons will show you around. It's fascinating!"

"How does that help us?" Philomena asked.

"It's easier to show you than tell you. We need to find the door. Let's not forget that little painting when we leave," Noshi said.

Noshi, Philomena, and Daisy went to separate corners of the room searching for any crack in the stone.

"Found it!" Daisy called out in excitement a short while later.

"Hey, how'd you find it so fast?" Philomena asked.

"I'm built low to the ground, and I saw light coming from underneath," Daisy said, pointing to a very narrow slit of light at the base of the wall.

It took all three of them to pry the door open. "He probably never used this door. He probably just hopped into one of his paintings, taking the express train instead of the local," said Philomena slyly.

Noshi scanned the little stone room again and concluded, "Not a bad setup. It looks like his life revolved around his art and his travels."

"Rama, the flashing lights hurt my eyes!" MacCaully shouted.

They were now experiencing the strobe light effect of the transit process, which was disconcerting for the young girl.

Rama replied supportively, "Jump on my back, dear child."

MacCaully grabbed hold of Rama's thick fur and hoisted herself onto his back.

Just then they were catapulted through some kind of threshold and landed in a tent-like structure. Rama managed to land upright, with MacCaully holding tightly to his neck.

The place felt strangely familiar to Rama. "This is a Native American teepee," he whispered.

"How do you know that?" asked MacCaully.

Rama smiled at her and replied, "The animal hides skillfully sewn together and their sound as the wind moves through them vaguely remind me of a life lived long ago, perhaps."

"Is this where we came from?" MacCaully asked, looking at the painting on the easel in the center of the teepee, depicting an image of a vast room with windows letting in a beautiful light through warm-colored curtains.

"I think we entered Grady's painting and arrived here. And now standing before us is a painting of a different subject," suggested Rama.

"Will we be able to get back home?" MacCaully asked anxiously.

"We'll know more once we explore where we are... and maybe even *when* we are," Rama said before cautiously striding outside the tent with MacCaully clinging to his neck. "Let's climb that boulder over there and get a better look," he added.

Rama began walking toward the big rock and then stopped dead in his tracks. Spellbound in the middle of a field of tall grasses, he had a strong instinct to face the teepee they had come from, and when he did he noticed another teepee next to it. "We are in Grady's stolen painting," he said in awe.

MacCaully looked at the boulder and asked, "Then where is the Indian man who was on the rock?"

Rama smiled at his young charge and replied, "There are more questions than answers today." Rama decided to head back to the teepees, quite sure that they held the answers being sought. As they approached the second teepee, Rama nudged the animal hide open with his nose, and they entered.

In the center of the teepee stood an easel supporting a large painting. "It's just black," declared MacCaully as she leaned forward on Rama's furry neck.

Though it appeared to be a picture of a black void, Rama noticed that the painting had a sense of space and dimension, with shades of black and dark gray, along with a hint of gold color that looked like faint window light. Rama looked in the lower right corner of the painting and there, rendered very small and barely noticeable, was the signature of the artist, Temporani, alongside his characteristic golden rays pointing upward.

"Do you think my brother followed us into the stolen painting, Rama?" asked MacCaully.

"He may well have. But without a companion it could be a terrifying experience for him," he said gravely.

MacCaully did not want to admit it, but she was worried about her brother getting lost in time and space.

The way Temporani looked at it, he had a simple choice: follow the boy into the El Ortiz Hotel painting or go to one of his sanctuaries. He knew he'd have to retrieve the boy at some point, but doing so could compromise his secrets. He opted to gain solace from the unnerving events of the past day by being around his paintings in Beecham's Pullman car.

With that thought, he leapt into the black void. The frail old man in the fedora, wearing an ancient backpack containing artist materials, was transiting from the plains of North Dakota and the Sioux Nation of 1830, having left his trusted friend Nahimana. There were times during his transits when he felt completely at peace and renewed. During this transit, however, he was deeply troubled by the spectral bridge on which he'd seen the other travelers and by the fact that they apparently had his cursed little painting of the temple. "Did they have the knowledge to communicate with the painting, and what would that mean?" he asked himself. Before long, the familiar stroboscopic effect ceased, and Temporani braced himself for reentry through the portal, taking solace in knowing that the only other human soul he trusted with his life would be there to greet him.

Temporani had known for many, many years that Lamy, New Mexico, was a nexus of time-space disruptions, a situation he had taken advantage of. Beecham's old Hamilton Pullman car was one of the epicenters of this queer phenomenon. It sat unassumingly on a section of abandoned track, unused for many years. And it wasn't likely that anyone aboard the daily Amtrak trains running the tracks east to Chicago or west to Los Angeles could imagine the secrets of time and space existing within it.

In the dim light of the Hamilton's interior coach, Temporani felt his way down its long center corridor. He passed multiple works of art, all resting on wooden easels on either side of the endless hallway, paintings of places he'd yet to explore and of landscapes that were like old friends, graced as they were with some Giallo di Napoli pigment. Temporani chuckled as he remembered when he had first discovered just how long Beecham's Pullman car actually was. From the outside, it appeared to be a regulation-size, eighty-foot Pullman car, but upon entering its interior he had become aware, with Beecham's assistance, that the car was three miles long, requiring about an hour to walk from front to back. It was the pronounced time-space anomaly in Beecham's Pullman car that had provided Temporani with more than enough storage for the majority of his life's work, now tucked away in the hidden Pullman car sitting on a length of abandoned track.

Upon meeting him for the first time, Temporani considered Beecham a somewhat befuddled loner, an old man tied to his train, all factors that had played into Temporani's plan. Having discovered the time-space anomaly in the Pullman car, Temporani had asked Beecham to walk with him to the very back of the car. In a tentative voice, Beecham had admitted sheepishly, "I've never walked all the way back there. One day many years ago, when I was a much younger man, I got the courage up to walk a ways back there. I probably went about a hundred yards before I realized something was very unusual. I started hearing voices from the past and got spooked. From that time on, I never went farther back there."

While walking together in the darkness, Temporani had encouraged Beecham to converse with him, figuring it might relax the old man. "I've been a train aficionado for many, many years. I was born on a train like this one way back in '36. I vowed that if I ever got the chance I'd buy one of 'em to live in. Bought this one at auction about forty years ago, and I've lived in it ever since. Only I didn't know it was as special as it turned out to be. In 1943, President Franklin Delano Roosevelt slept in the upper berth just down the corridor," Beecham had said.

"Tell me, Beecham, have you brought anyone else back here?" Temporani had asked innocently.

"Local kids always want to get a look inside, but I just let them see my sitting room at the front. And when I leave I always lock my metal door," Beecham had explained.

The farther back they walked into the Pullman car, the more agitated Beecham had become. To make him feel a little more comfortable, Temporani had leaned his shoulder into him.

"What do you do, sir?" Beecham had asked.

Adjusting his fedora, Temporani had replied, "I am an artist and art collector, and I have a proposition for you. You have a lot of space—much more than you will ever use. I would like to make the back of your Pullman car a museum of sorts."

Beecham had stopped walking and asked, "Like an art museum? But then nobody else gets to see the artwork."

With a twinkle in his eye, Temporani had replied, "Precisely. I am willing to offer you an annual rent, payable in gold coins on the first of each year, for the use of the back of your Pullman car." The feeble light from the nearly blacked-out windows of the forgotten train had cast a faint dingy yellow light upon the corridor floor. Beecham was a trusting man, and though his intuition had told him to be wary of making deals with this mysterious man with the backpack he finally agreed to Temporani's terms.

It had taken them an entire hour to walk the full length of Beecham's Pullman car, and when they had at last reached the back of it Beecham took off his old pinstriped train hat, scratched his head, and asked, "Mr. Temporani, do you have an explanation for why my eighty-foot train car has taken us this long to walk through?"

Temporani had relaxed his highly attuned survival instincts just a bit and answered honestly, "There are places on earth that don't operate in normal ways with regard to time. They are like 'pools' of time disruption that you can dive into and out of once you locate them. Time and space are stretched in this Pullman car, though the exact reason remains a mystery. I am practiced in locating such time-space anomalies, and I know that one must have a strong mind to confront these challenging realms of disrupted time."

Daisy, Philomena, and Noshi, who held the painting with its golden rays, stealthily moved through the upper floor of the Scottish Rite Temple.

"What if someone sees us, Noshi?" whispered Philomena.

"We'll just say we're waiting for our host to show us around," Noshi replied.

They crept around a corner and saw a flight of stairs. Along the stairway were dusty old portraits of men wearing curious hats.

"These are Masons?" asked Daisy.

"Yes. I toured this temple a few years ago. I'd heard about the theater and asked permission to see it," explained Noshi.

"They have their own theater here?" Philomena asked in a surprised voice.

"Yes, and it's like nothing I've ever seen before. I was told that they actually built the whole temple around the theater because it was so complex, with many moving backdrops held by wires attached to the ceiling," replied Noshi.

They descended two more flights of stairs, with portraits of Masons in hats staring down at them. The painting's golden rays were illuminating some of the portraits in grotesque ways.

Noshi thought to himself, "Curious that there's no one around. Could it be closed today?"

Finally, they reached the ground floor, where Noshi pushed open a set of black doors to reveal a large, bowl-like theater with a stage at its base. Daisy's fur tingled. She was amazed at all the enormous hand-painted back-drops and different massive hanging murals suspended above her head. She mused to herself, "There's something mysterious about these paintings. I think time and space are porous here as well. It's like the painted murals are of different realities." She felt like she had when her train pulled into the Lamy station and she saw the abandoned train.

Her eyes fixed on the last in the line of hanging back-drops; it was the only one that did not depict a conventional landscape but rather a brilliant lapis lazuli sky filled with a myriad of stars. Below the star field there appeared to be twelve throne chairs arranged in a semicircle above their heads, and below those were blue ripples of water.

It almost looked like the chairs were suspended in the shallow water. Daisy's fur tingled, and she thought, "These fancy chairs are for some very special people. I think a meeting of extraordinary beings will happen here, but what is the reason for this gathering and what will they look like?"

Noshi and Philomena joined Daisy at the back of the stage. "Daisy, why are you getting that far-off look again?" Philomena asked.

Daisy replied, "This mural may be a piece of the puzzle, but what does it mean?"

Noshi remarked, "It feels like something important is about to happen in the mural, with the stars and the chairs all in alignment. I'll bet you a box of the world's most expensive oil paints that the missing piece to the puzzle—and the one that will return us home—is a connection between our painting and this mural."

Daisy looked at Temporani's painting and then at the mural and had a revelation. "The twelve faint stars in the painting match the twelve stars in the mural!" she exclaimed.

Noshi and Philomena could see that Daisy was now going into a trance-like state, as she had when they first touched the little painting in the dark corridor of the El Ortiz Hotel. Daisy began to sway from side to side as she said, "There will be a meeting of twelve souls here at the Scottish Rite Temple. We three are to take our rightful places on the throne-chairs as part of some council. But I foresee a period of darkness and tribulation before we are ready to claim our seats on this council, which, I sense, is to decide no less than the fate of humanity."

"We must buy you a new pair of glasses when we return—these are badly cracked. I want you to read to me forever," MacCaully said sweetly.

"This pair of glasses will do just fine for now, my dear," Rama said. He stood in front of the black void painting, with MacCaully holding tight to his furry neck.

MacCaully reached down and held Rama's broken glasses close to his big brown eyes. Though apprehensive, she knew she would always be safe with her llama. "Why are we going into this black painting and not the one in the other teepee?" MacCaully asked.

"A feeling, my child," replied Rama. "I am consulting my heart and not my mind. You know I've lived many lives, and the one thing I've understood is that when you consult your heart instead of your head you allow for the possibility of magic. Your heart is like an infinite well of knowing; your mind is a blunt tool best attuned to survival. When you find the balance of the two opposed elements, you will have the very best of both worlds." MacCaully leaned forward and kissed Rama on his nose, and then they tumbled into the painting.

Rama loved the feeling of freedom he had while moving through nothingness as they traveled. He detected many languages faintly spoken by numerous voices during the journey, though he could only recognize a few of them. MacCaully felt safe riding on Rama's back, and holding his glasses up to his eyes made her feel useful.

They arrived in nearly total darkness, with only enough light to a see a few steps in front and around them. They heard the familiar mournful wail of a train in the distance. Walking forward cautiously, Rama veered a little as the faint light shone from a painting on an easel. Without stopping, he ventured further along and came upon another painting on an easel.

"Rama, where are we?" MacCaully asked.

"It seems to be a gallery of paintings in a dark corridor."

"You mean like a museum?" she asked.

Rama smiled and replied, "Yes, only the owner of the gallery seems to not want visitors."

Following his instincts, Rama moved to the other side of the narrow corridor they were navigating and saw even more paintings on easels all lined up. The distance between paintings was roughly the distance between the circles of light faintly illuminating them. "No one going perfectly straight down the middle of the corridor would know these paintings existed," he thought.

As they walked in silence looking at paintings on either side of the corridor, they heard the muffled sound of a train screeching to a stop. "It sounds like we are close to a train station," MacCaully said excitedly.

Then they heard a woman's voice call out, "Augustus, Orson, come here now!"

Rama tilted his head toward the noise, and MacCaully strained to listen as well.

"The train is leaving. Come here immediately!" the woman now shouted with urgency.

"It sounds like the woman is calling her sons," Rama inferred.

Then they heard one of the boys call back, "Mother, can we bring this dog with us?"

"Absolutely not. Get out of the hotel right now and board this train! And grab your brother Orson," the mother shouted.

"She said *hotel*. Wasn't there an old hotel that stood next to the train station in Lamy way back when?" asked Rama.

"Yes, the El Ortiz Hotel. Grady knew about it; he saw old pictures of it," MacCaully said.

They walked at a more rapid pace, looking at the many paintings resting on easels. Most were landscapes, some with ancient ruins like Doric columns and amphitheaters; all shared a beautiful inner glow. Suddenly they heard footsteps coming toward them and were confronted by two old men.

"I wondered when this might happen," Temporani said in the direction of the llama and the girl riding it.

Rama stared at the old man, who was dressed in old-fashioned attire—tailored wool pants, Italian-looking shoes, a brown fedora, and a backpack—very different from that of his companion. "I am Rama, and the child is MacCaully," he said.

"I know the girl," the other man shouted in recognition. He took a step closer and asked, "How did you get back here?"

MacCaully recognized him and remarked, "Hi, Beecham. I didn't know you collected paintings."

Beecham stammered, "It's kind of a new interest."

"We were deposited here," Rama answered simply.

MacCaully lovingly kissed Rama's neck, jumped off him, and asked Beecham, "Is this your Pullman car? Are we home?"

Beecham smiled and answered, "Yes, you are home, but where have you been?"

"We were in a grassy field with teepees; before that we were in the Cerro Colorado mine; but now we're here. It's all pretty mixed up," she explained.

Rama was trying to read the man with the fedora hat. His wizened old face was tightening, his jaw clenching, and his eyes getting squinty. Rama decided to follow his intuition and asked, "Are you the creator of all these paintings?"

The man's eyes widened in surprise. "I am an art collector, and I happen to know the painter of these works," he stated.

"Let's go outside. I want to see the daylight!" Mac-Caully said, excitedly.

Beecham took her hand in his and said, with a smile, "We have a long walk ahead of us. I'll try to explain."

Before they left, MacCaully ran back to Rama, gave him a big hug, and whispered, with tears in her eyes, "I will only go on adventures with you, Rama."

Rama teared up as well and said to her softly, "The universe is benevolent, and we will always find our way home as long as we listen to our hearts."

Temporani was fascinated with this llama, thinking that it carried itself in an almost imperial manner.

"Do you mind my asking a few questions of you, sir?" Rama inquired, thinking the little man was quite an anachronism in his vintage clothing. "Do you travel a lot, Mr. —?" he asked.

"Oh, forgive me. My name is Mr. Temporani," the old man said. "I do travel extensively, all over the world, looking for new artists to collect." Rama was sure this little man standing before him was the artist who had created the portal painting into which he and MacCaully had tumbled.

They began walking slowly down the corridor toward the front of the train and could still hear Beecham and MacCaully chatting excitedly up ahead of them. "Do you believe in past lives, Mr. Temporani?" inquired Rama. He had the strongest feeling that Temporani had many secrets befitting a man he sensed was not restricted to living in conventional linear time.

"There are moments when I feel that I've experienced quite a few past lives," Temporani replied slyly.

Rama sensed that Temporani had been around for many, many lifetimes. In a way, they were kindred spirits, only up until recently all Rama's lives had been lived sequentially following rebirths, unlike Temporani's. Then Rama risked another bold question: "Would you consider doing a custom painting for me?"

Temporani stopped walking and looked up at Rama. He shifted the weight of his backpack on his shoulders as though the question made him uncomfortable. "Why do you think I am the creator of these paintings?" he asked.

Rama replied, "Let's not play games. We are both travelers—and, in a sense, spiritual brothers. In my sleep, I still travel in dreams to my past lives and relive them. I try to glean the lessons to be learned when I've faltered or caused pain to others. I can recount lifetimes as a king, a slave, a politician, a day laborer, an artist, a thief, a soldier, and a scientist. Just as you have discovered arcane methods of travel in time and space, in effect cheating the linear flow of time, I wish to cheat as well. Most recently, I have been assigned a lifetime as a beast of burden. You, Mr. Temporani, are the vehicle for my transformation and transcendence. Will you paint a picture to my specifications?"

Temporani chuckled as he realized he was in the presence of no ordinary llama. "Rama, I have a counteroffer for you: I will paint a picture for you in trade for some help with a problem. Things are getting increasingly messy in the temporal continuum, and I would like your assistance in cleaning up some loose ends."

"You have my conditional yes, but I must ask you to explain the nature of the mess," Rama replied shrewdly.

"There is a teenager lost in transit. I know where he landed, but I don't know what he's doing or if he's injured or has injured others," Temporani said gravely.

"I know this boy," Rama said bluntly. "His family owns me. He stole your Native American man painting from the Pink Garter Saloon not far from here. It is the painting my young friend and I first entered—your painting."

"Will you help me find him and return him home?" Temporani asked.

Rama sensed he had leverage in this negotiation and pressed the artist. "I know how the boy thinks. I will help you retrieve him on the condition that I be allowed to travel with you."

Temporani narrowed his wrinkled eyes and made a mental note to never underestimate this llama. They were now almost at the front of the train. Temporani had begun to relax his wariness around Rama, understanding that this unusual llama with the multitude of past lives could be a worthy traveling partner. "You are aware that Lamy, New Mexico, represents a kind of rupture in time. The normal rules of linear time and space don't apply here," Temporani advised.

Rama replied, "I've known this for some time now."

# CHAPTER 13

Daisy glanced up again at the amazing network of backdrops suspended a hundred feet above them by heavy cables. She tried to suppress the feeling of being lost in a world of puzzles and clues but few answers. She derived strength and comfort in knowing that she was with her traveling companions. She recalled Noshi saying that being an Imagination Warrior means going your own way, and that it can be a lonely journey at times because so few choose this path in life. She took a deep breath and resolved to face the next challenge with grit, determination, and the courage to imagine all possibilities, all paths. She reflected on the cold rainy night long ago when Mrs. Z had rescued her at the animal shelter. "There is a plan for all of us. We simply need to trust in ourselves," Daisy thought, with assurance.

Then she recalled her magical second night in New Mexico, huddled with her new friends atop Noshi's mountain. She vowed never to forget their shared experience of the myriad stars from which filaments of light touched the earth and interconnected all things. She had come so far from her perch atop her purple pillow looking down from the bay window in New York City, observing but not participating in life. "The power of imagination is real. I've seen it in action," she thought to herself.

Philomena could see that Daisy was reflecting and said, "Daisy, I know you're chewing on something. What is it?"

Just then Daisy had a revelation and said, "I've come to realize that we all have a lot of power but don't know it. And we are all connected but don't know it."

Philomena then blurted out cynically, "If that's true, how come we can't simply wish ourselves home, Daisy?"

Daisy tilted her head as if trying to decipher a distant sound and replied, "Maybe there is a grand plan for us all, something we don't know about, something beyond our ability to see."

Noshi smiled and said, "Your powers of perception are growing daily, Daisy. Supposedly I am the head Imagination Warrior, who talks about the powers of imagination and how, if we continue to develop them responsibly, we elevate ourselves and empower ourselves to walk the path less taken. But I accept your conclusion. We truly are the captains of our destinies!"

Daisy purred in appreciation of Noshi's acknowledgment but felt compelled to say cautiously," I believe all this is true, but I can't shake the feeling that we are being led in mysterious ways that we cannot yet fathom. As much as I like the idea that we are in control, Noshi, I am positive there is a silent, invisible hand steering our ship and that the little painting is a part of it. We've already surmised that Temporani was not able to access its mysteries, but maybe we can."

"Why can't this gathering happen now?" asked a frustrated Philomena.

"And who painted that mural above us?" Daisy asked.

Noshi looked up at the mural of stars and chairs as if he were searching for something then replied, "The temple guide said the landscapes were done seventy or eighty years ago by commissioned local Santa Fe artists, but the stars and chairs mural was done long before the others."

"How long ago, Noshi?" asked Daisy.

Noshi continued, "The guide said temple records state that this painting was done many hundreds of years ago by an Italian artist.

"Could it have been done by Temporani?" asked Daisy inquisitively.

"Wouldn't that be a funny little wrinkle—that above the theater, three stories below his little hidden stone studio in the Scottish Rite Temple, hangs a painting he did five hundred years ago. This could be why I think there needs to be a dialogue between the two paintings, particularly if Temporani chose to apply some of his special Naples yellow pigment to the mural as well," said Noshi.

"Imagine two paintings created by the same artist, separated by five hundred years or more," Daisy added.

"Well, we can imagine all we want, but what are we going to do about it?" asked Philomena, frustrated. Daisy was quiet for a while, and the others knew she was working on something. She sat directly underneath the giant mural and looked up to see it fifty feet above their heads. She rocked slowly back and forth on her hind legs, then said, "I sense that the water at the bottom of the mural represents a challenge for the people who would claim their throne-chairs, an obstacle to overcome before these chosen ones can ascend to carry out their responsibilities."

Philomena seemed a little skeptical about Daisy's theory and asked, "Now that you've figured this out, can you tell us why these twelve people will be meeting?"

Daisy smiled and replied, "If you stand under this thing long enough, answers eventually come to you! I think the twelve stars above them represent a cosmic alignment of very powerful entities. This mural reminds me of a tarot card, with its symbolism and potential consequences. I sense that the forces arrayed against the alliance of twelve people are quite strong and very old. But I think they may be threatened by this alliance of twelve and will defend themselves vigorously."

"Daisy, is there a way we can get our little Temporani painting to talk to the bigger Temporani mural?" asked Philomena.

Still in her trance-like state, Daisy surprised Philomena and Noshi with her response. She touched the little painting with her paw to connect with its power then revealed, "Our painting is calling out for another painting so that it can become animate. It's not the one above us but a different painting."

"Daisy, could the other painting be my painting of the Native American princess into which we fell?" asked Noshi.

Daisy sat more upright as though something important was about to occur. She then revealed, "That is correct, Noshi. Your painting of the young princess is preparing to become animate, to come alive."

"What does that mean?" asked Philomena.

"Noshi's creation back in his Lamy studio is awaiting a sign to awaken."

"How is this possible?" asked Noshi, incredulously.

Daisy's fur tingled, indicating that these wild predictions were true. "From what I can comprehend," she began, "through this process a rare event will occur involving the confluence of two strong forces, imagination and intention. The little Temporani painting has begun to reveal some information about this alchemy. Just as Philomena and I came together to solve a mystery, so the little painting wants to join with Noshi's creation. But unfortunately there are obstacles to this, foretold in the mural hanging above us."

Visibly upset by this news, Philomena shouted, "Daisy, I just want to go home!" Then she sat down rebelliously on the stage floor, under the heavy mural ominously suspended above them.

Noshi went into action, saying, "Warrior Philomena, it sounds like we have just this one challenge before us, and, as selfish as this sounds, I'm really excited to see my painting come alive!"

Daisy comforted Philomena and said encouragingly, "Noshi is right: we must meet this challenge. Then we get to go home." She pawed the small painting so that it was between them and advised, "Let's sit down and concentrate on the little painting and the forces that may want to join with Noshi's painting."

As they did this, the three warriors rocketed through the void of the unknown again, now beginning to understand that the little painting had a plan for them—that with it Temporani had unwittingly created a powerful engine of thought that he himself had not entirely understood.

Philomena's thoughts drifted to an earlier, happy time when she and her dad would meander along the path that ran alongside the railroad tracks in Lamy, following their noses as they pretended to be archaeologists in search of ancient treasures that might lie tantalizingly just beneath the surface of the earth. From time to time, when she needed comfort, she had reflected on those magical times with her father. She'd remember the way he would walk, not in a straight line but in a kind of gentle arc and then bend down to inspect something he'd seen in the dirt. She would remember his enthusiasm at finding a piece of broken pottery and the funny little sound he'd make when he realized it came from the El Ortiz Hotel lunchroom. She thought to herself, "If I could just hold these moments close to my heart forever, always remember they are part of me and my dad, and never forget how special I felt walking side by side with him and sharing adventures, with no particular plan and the whole long day ahead of us."

At that moment, everything changed. Daisy was the first to comprehend what was happening. Out of the corner of her eye, she saw a flash of brilliant light shaped like a bullet approaching them from behind, traveling even faster than they were. Daisy had just enough time to scream, "Watch out!"

The silver bullet was upon them in an instant. Philomena had no time to react. She clutched Daisy tightly with all her might, but the bullet seemed to possess an irresistible gravitational force, pulling her and Daisy away from Noshi.

Noshi looked with horror as Philomena and Daisy were violently wrenched away from him and absorbed into the bullet that was now racing ahead of him into the void. He tried desperately to think of something he could do to help his fellow warriors. Suddenly, he knew what to do. "I'll redirect the painting's rays straight ahead. Hopefully, I'll lock onto their time bullet," he thought.

In the fading light, Marco watched as the remainder of his young crew jumped into their four-wheel-drive vehicles and left the dig site. He had wanted some time to himself to process what had happened, and he was grateful for the solitude. He paced the dig site, looking at their work of the last few months. They'd painstakingly uncovered a remarkably intact triceratops fossil from a remote hillside and named it Trini. He had been so excited that he phoned his daughter about the fossil.

But then he himself had made a discovery less than one hundred feet away in a cave: a mysterious wooden cylinder that he had not told his students about. At that point, he had not been sure if he was a paleontologist or an archaeologist, a dilemma that would have thrilled his daughter. He could imagine her rooting around, getting dirty, enjoying discovering such an ancient container, deciphering its meaning, and trying to determine why it had been placed in that cave. "What a great father-daughter project that would be!" he thought.

A curious set of circumstances had led to its discovery. He'd taken a midday break from the tedious process of brushing away the detritus of millions of years to reveal the bones of Trini, meandered away from the dig site, and literally stumbled into a low hill, shaking the wooden cylinder loose. He had picked it up and studied it. The wood was weathered and had deep fissures running the length of it. The cylinder was about a foot long and four inches wide. The top was hinged like a modern bank vacuum tube. Gently, he had attempted to open it by turning the top. To his astonishment, the wooden top gave way, and he had cautiously beamed his flashlight into it. Tentatively reaching in, he had pulled out what looked like a rolled-up cotton canvas that had been treated with some sort of preserving oil. He'd carefully unrolled the canvas and seen a painting of a landscape with ancient ruins, the foreground dominated by an upturned stone woman's head. "Looks like ancient ruins in fog. For some reason, I always expect pictures of archaeological ruins to show them in the light of a setting sun," he had thought.

Right away one of his students had shouted, "Oh, intrepid professor, where are you?" He had quickly rolled the painting up back into the cylinder and hidden the cylinder in the dirt near the cave's entrance. Now he returned to the cave, retrieved the cylinder, and placed it in his backpack.

Philomena could not believe her eyes. There, standing on the spectral bridge, sharing the same time-space bullet, was Grady, shaking uncontrollably. "What are you doing here?" she shouted incredulously.

"Hey, you jumped into my express train! You and your cat!" replied a surly Grady. "I've been tossed all over the place, from picture to picture."

Daisy thought to herself, "Here's the invisible hand of our painting working its strange magic again. Finding Grady in this infinite space is like hitting a bullet with another bullet traveling at the speed of thought."

"What happened to you, Grady?" Philomena demanded.

Grady pulled his hands away from his face. He had tears in his eyes. "I jumped into the painting from the Pink Garter Saloon," he confessed. "Then I got pushed into another painting by some old man wearing a gangster hat who said he was an artist."

"What did he look like?" asked Daisy.

Grady self-consciously wiped the tears from his face and said, "A small old man wearing a leather backpack. He talked kind of funny, like out of an old movie."

Philomena and Daisy gasped. "Temporani," they said simultaneously.

"We know his paintings. We've been diving in and out of them for what feels like months," added Daisy.

Grady's eyes looked like teacup saucers. "Did you guys land in the teepee, like me?" he asked.

"Yeah, we did all that," Philomena said, a note of pride in her voice.

"Well, try time-space traveling all alone on the ghost bridge looking at stars all around you and hearing scary sounds and never knowing where you'll wind up," he said defensively.

For the first time ever, Philomena felt sorry for Grady. She'd known he was angry and a little mean, but now she understood what he'd just been through. She'd had Daisy and Noshi as trusted companions on her transits, while Grady had had no one. She now realized that she and Grady were not so different and that the things they shared were more important than their differences, that they had much common ground with which to build a better friendship.

"Hey, we're experiencing the strobe light effect now," declared Daisy.

As it increased in intensity, Grady inched closer to Philomena and Daisy. "I hate this part. It also happened last time to me," he said. He recalled a time when all he wanted to do was escape his parents, his life, everything. He'd seen a picture in an old magazine of an airplane and thought to himself, "I wonder what it would feel like to be getting away from everything you know, traveling to some distant land where everything is new and different."

Philomena and Daisy, who were familiar enough with the transit by this point to know that it was almost complete, braced themselves for what was to come. Philomena surprised herself by saying to Grady, "Keep close to us. We never know how we're going to land."

Grady self-consciously leaned into Philomena, hoping she wouldn't notice. Philomena grabbed Daisy in her arms and held her tightly. Daisy thought to herself, "That's strange. There's no warm air or sounds present like during the other transits we've been through."

And then their reality changed drastically as they were deposited into a thick fog. The three travelers stood silent and motionless, not knowing what to do. Philomena missed Noshi's sense of humor and perspective. He always managed to lighten the mood, whatever the circumstance. Hopefully he was okay.

"Where in the world did we land?" she asked, as confidently as she could manage. Then she looked behind them in the direction of the painting through which they'd traveled and exclaimed, "Oh no, there's no painting here!"

Grady, Philomena, and Daisy stared at an easel obscured by the heavy fog, with no painting resting upon it. This confirmed Daisy's suspicion that the current transit would be different from all the others.

The fog was becoming so thick that they could barely see one another, and Grady started to shake again. Philomena grabbed him by the shoulders and said, "Our friend Noshi always knew we'd all be okay in our travels. To reassure us, he'd often say, 'We are unharmed, we are healthy, and we are together.' So calm down, Grady."

Grady took a deep breath and replied, "You guys are all I've got right now. We gotta stick together."

Philomena scooped up Daisy in her arms, and they walked shoulder to shoulder into the fog.

Soon Grady remarked, as optimistically as he could, "Look, the fog is letting up further ahead."

The fog dispersed just enough for them to see that they were walking on sand, sparkling somewhat as it caught light from above, brightening their mood.

"Grady, got a watch?" Philomena asked.

"Yeah, my old Swiss Army one," he replied.

"Let's keep walking toward the brightest part of the fog while keeping track of our elapsed time," said Philomena.

"Okay, so the empty easel is our ground zero, and we'll explore from there," Grady added.

Relieved at Grady's cooperation, Philomena thought to herself, "I wonder if he's going to go back to his old depressed self when we return home."

"Ten minutes now," Grady said as they continued walking in the sand through the fog.

Then above them they saw lightning illuminating the fog and soon heard the sound of muffled thunder reverberating. Philomena looked up and declared, "We really need to find shelter."

Daisy sensed something ahead of them, just beyond their range of vision. "Hold up," she said cautiously.

Philomena and Grady stopped walking and peered into the fog. Something big was looming up in front of them.

Grady instinctively pressed his shoulder into Philomena's. They moved slowly toward the object. Philomena tripped over something, fell to the sand, and dropped Daisy. Grady managed to avoid stumbling over it and helped her up.

"It's a fragment of stone. Looks like part of a snake," Philomena said. Picking it up, she realized that it was actually part of a giant sculpture.

They moved closer to the object as a light rain began to fall through the fog. "This is not a good trend," Daisy muttered under her breath as she shook off the rain.

Bravely, they approached the object towering ahead of them. The fog parted just enough for them to see what it was. "It's an enormous head facing upward!" Philomena exclaimed as the three travelers were confronted with a six-foot carved stone head of a woman.

"Where's the rest of the body?" asked Grady.

"Probably buried beneath this sand," said Daisy.

Philomena kept staring at the statue's head through the rain. "There's something familiar about this statue. I gotta figure this out," she ruminated.

Daisy leapt from Philomena's arms onto the statue's prominent nose. The surface was slick with rain, causing her to slip onto the statue's cheek.

Eyeing the landscape around them, Grady said in a concerned voice, "The fog is beginning to lift. We should really look for cover."

Philomena was still transfixed by the statue of the woman. "It's the Medusa. Instead of hair, she has snakes. It's an old Greek myth," she announced.

"That myth always scared the hell out of me. What the heck is it doing here?" asked Grady.

"Wait a minute!" Philomena said excitedly. "I got it... I know why this is here!"

The sand beneath their feet was getting saturated with rain. "Oh no. I think the water is rising, and we are totally exposed! You can play out your archaeology fantasy later. We need to reach higher ground, and fast!" shouted Grady.

Daisy was afforded an elevated perspective as she climbed up to the stone woman's forehead. Once there, she peered through the rain and declared, "The fog is lifting, but I see ripples of water coming this way. And I see another structure or something in the distance."

Meanwhile, Philomena seemed to be frozen, incapable of action. She told herself, "I was thinking about that day many years ago when my dad and I went looking for treasures as if we were archaeologists!"

As the fog thinned, Daisy shouted, "Looks like an airplane in the distance, maybe a hundred yards away. We should try to reach it while we can still see it."

Daisy jumped off the statue and into Philomena's arms. Then Grady, Philomena, and Daisy waded through the rising water toward the thing in the distance that looked like an airplane.

As they approached it, Grady felt a sense of déjà vu and said, "I know this aircraft! It's a de Havilland Comet. Look at the way the jet engines are integrated into the wing. Futuristic, right? This was the first commercial jet that flew cross country. It was light years ahead of its time!"

They could hear the sound of water moving toward them. It had now reached up to Philomena's knees. "Hurry, we gotta find a way into his thing," she shouted.

Grady replied, "Follow me. The fuselage is leaning. We can enter through the rear door."

The rain was lashing their faces as they raced to enter the old jet. Grady hopped onto the wing and reached a hand down to pull Philomena and Daisy up on the wing. While they stood on the listing wing of the old aircraft staring through the rain with trepidation, the fog retreated, and they were horrified by what they saw.

Philomena held Daisy close and, gazing toward the horizon, saw an endless ocean stretching out before them. With a troubled look on her face, Daisy said, "This whole place is unstable—the fog, lightning and thunder, the ocean moving toward us, and these bizarre artifacts, remnants from other times. I sense that this is an unbalanced world. It is trying to tell us something important."

Philomena had been struggling silently with their dire situation and sat down on the leaning wing of the Comet, dangling her legs over the edge as she looked vacantly out at the endless sea. She started to cry. The water was now lapping up onto the edge of the Comet's listing wing.

Daisy nestled into Philomena's lap and said, "I feel so alone."

Trying to be sympathetic, Grady replied, "Welcome to my world. I always feel alone. Listen, the water can't rise forever. Chances are it'll level off."

Philomena lowered her head and said under her breath, "I miss him."

Grady responded, "Your dad?"

Philomena nodded and wiped tears from her eyes. "The stone statue back there reminded me of him."

"Doesn't anyone want to get out of the rain?" Grady asked, trying to change the subject.

Daisy shouted, "This place seems to be a kind of giant amplifier. You were telling us about the time you and your dad went walking together, pretending to be archaeologists, right?"

"Wait, you mean I created the Medusa statue?" Philomena asked, incredulously.

"I think you did create it. And Grady, how did you know about this aircraft we're on right now?" Daisy asked confidently.

Grady sat down next to Philomena and explained, "All I ever wanted was to be free of my family and life in Lamy. Late at night I'd look at old airplane magazines because I love seeing the old aircraft. They seemed so glamorous. They flew in the sky above all the trouble down below—they were free. I needed to believe there was freedom somewhere."

Daisy jumped in and continued to build her case. "So you, Philomena, and you, Grady, have created these artifacts. The stone Medusa and the Comet aircraft come from two powerful forces: memory and imagination. They reflect for you, Philomena, memory of a special shared moment with your dad, and for you, Grady, memory of an aircraft that symbolizes freedom from family strife."

Grady stood up and faced the de Havilland Comet with his arms outstretched and stated proudly, "I must have an awesome imagination to have re-created this entire aircraft! I wish it could fly us outta here."

Philomena said begrudgingly under her breath, "We may have to include you in our tribe."

Intrigued, Grady turned to face his fellow travelers and asked, "You have a tribe?"

Noshi hit his head hard in the wet sand, but he managed to protect the painting upon impact. Slowly, he stood up, wiping the sand from his face, and began to assess his situation. "It's nighttime with low-hanging fog; I'm standing in wet sand. I don't think this is a positive development," he thought to himself. He whirled around and saw that he was entirely alone in this dark world, with no fellow Imagination Warriors or familiar portal painting on an easel.

It began to rain lightly, a kind of misting rain that would be pleasant just about anywhere else, but here seemed ominous. Many unanswered questions crowded his mind. "What happens when this painting gets wet? Are my friends in this sandy, wet region, too, and are they safe? How do I return home, or anywhere else for that matter, without a painting to tumble into?" he wondered.

He resolved to find shelter, worried that since the little painting he was carrying might be his only exit from this place he'd better keep it as dry as possible.

But first he decided to risk getting the painting a little wet in the light rain to see if it could illuminate anything that would help him. He held it up as if it were a beacon, beaming its intense golden rays outward. The beams fixed on what appeared to be a large rock in the distance. He welcomed the sight, thinking it might provide some elevation above the water, and set out in its direction. The fog was dense, and the painting's beam bounced back toward him, making it difficult to navigate in the sand. By the time he reached the rock, he was ankle-deep in water. He started to climb the slick rock, gripping whatever handholds he could find. Then just as he breathed a sigh of relief, thinking he was now up about six feet from the rising waters, he fully understood what he had climbed.

"It's a stone woman's face!" he thought. He gripped the nose with his left hand, holding the painting face-down to avoid getting it wet. He stared into the stone woman's sphinx-like haunting stone eyes as the thunder rumbled above him, and thought to himself, "This is a statue of the Medusa I visited in Didyma, Turkey, twenty years ago! I never forget a beautiful face!"

He looked down in horror as the waters continued to rise, now almost touching the stone woman's snake hair. The nighttime fog was beginning to dissipate, even though rains began to come down harder.

He decided to again try to use the painting as a beacon. Pointing it where the fog was thinnest, he saw another object looming ahead in the darkness, only partially visible. "I'm getting the strangest sense that this place is not real. It's more like a dream world with statues and sand and low-tide oceans," he thought.

He looked down in horror as whirlpools began to pop up all around him. He thought, "What next, a plague of locusts? I'm not so sure living in a painting is a good idea, especially since—" Then it dawned on him that the jolt he'd felt was a tremor moving the sand, rock, and ocean.

Suddenly, out of the fog he heard a voice scream, "Over here! Look down. In the boat."

Noshi looked out through the rain and, incredulous, saw a man piloting a small rowboat. He seemed to be practiced at avoiding the whirlpools that sprang up all around him.

"Climb down. The water will reach above the statue soon," advised the man.

Noshi began to climb down the slippery face of the Medusa, gazing at the man in the boat and thinking, "He looks like a caricature of every explorer I've ever seen: cargo pocket khakis, hiker's shirt with bellow pockets."

The man pulled his boat up against the Medusa's stone hair, and Noshi jumped in, holding the painting in his lap. "I see you managed to find my Medusa in the middle of all this water," the man said.

"*Your* Medusa? I thought it was *my* Medusa!" Noshi said almost comically.

The man continued, "I found an ancient painting in an equally ancient wooden cylinder, recognized that it was a painting of the Medusa, and now I'm here with you in the shadow of this stone Medusa. There doesn't seem to be much rhyme or reason to what happened."

Noshi smiled and said, "There may well be more rhyme and reason than you think. In any case, thank you for the timely rescue." Then Noshi saw that the man's right leg was heavily bandaged and asked, "What happened to your leg?"

"Broke it falling off the wet wing of an airplane," the man replied. "We need to row over there." The man pointed to the spot highlighted by the beam of Noshi's painting. "This world is unstable. I've been here for a couple of weeks and I've seen the changes," the man added gravely. "What's that in your lap, a favorite painting?"

Noshi smiled and replied, "It's been our traveling companion through a series of unusual adventures. It's looking for a kindred spirit, I think, and we're along for the ride. Sorry if this all sounds like a riddle. What's your name, sir?"

"Marco," the man answered. The rain was beginning to fill the boat with water, and Marco grimaced as he rowed toward the object in the ocean.

"Is this an ocean world?" Noshi asked.

"Yes and no. The water really only gets about eight feet high at high tide, but I think that may be changing now. I've noticed that the tide comes in faster and higher than just a week ago."

"A week ago? You've been here that long?" Noshi asked.

Marco nodded wearily.

Noshi looked up through the rain and, as he saw the object, gasped, "It's an airplane!"

While Marco navigated the boat under the plane's higher wing, Noshi noticed that the plane appeared to be an old jet engine aircraft, maybe from the fifties. "Why's it listing so much?" Noshi inquired.

"I guess the sand underneath is unstable," Marco replied. "It was more upright last week, another indication that this world is tearing apart."

The markings on the old jet indicated to Noshi that it was an English plane. "I read about this one! It's a de Havilland Comet. Went into service about 1950, I think. It was the first commercial jet airliner to cross the Atlantic," Noshi said. He could not help staring at Marco. Something about him was so familiar. "Where did you find the boat?" he asked.

"I think I imagined it" was Marco's extraordinary reply.

"Well, now you're talking my language. My friends and I have been bounced around multiple realities accessed through paintings that come alive!" revealed Noshi.

Marco rubbed his broken leg and said, "I'm a paleontologist by profession, and I fell into a painting as well, this one. I was at a dig site in North Dakota and I—"

"You're Philomena's dad!" Noshi shouted, cutting him off. "I just placed you by the way you dress—exactly like your daughter—and your resemblance to her!"

Surprised, Marco leaned toward Noshi and asked, "She's here on this water world?"

Noshi's expression turned serious. "I don't know. We were all traveling together—me, Philomena, and Daisy, a cat," he explained.

"Daisy is a cat?" asked Marco.

"Well, Daisy is Philomena's Imagination Warrior sister," Noshi replied matter-of-factly.

"Her imagination *what*?" Marco asked, in an exasperated voice.

Noshi could see that Marco was becoming distraught, and he wanted to reassure him. He took a deep breath and explained, "Your daughter is a very dynamic individual, and Daisy is her complement. They journeyed all the way up to my mountaintop in search of answers. They are seekers and adventurers, and you should be proud of them." Marco smiled and nodded.

Then Noshi continued, "Marco, I have a credo that I live my life by: When the imagination is engaged fully, we are free to create, free to live our lives courageously in our own individual fashion, unconcerned about the path the masses take. I built my house with my own two hands in a style that most people would consider bizarre and unorthodox. To me, there is great beauty in following your muse and intuition, wherever they take you. That is exactly how your brave daughter and Daisy live. I've never had children, but Philomena seems like my spiritual daughter, and I know she loves you very much, Marco. Looking at you and knowing your extraordinary daughter, I'm betting you're an Imagination Warrior, as well."

Marco's eyes teared up and he struggled to speak, but he was too overwhelmed by his emotions.

Noshi added, "Philomena and Daisy are my fellow Imagination Warriors. The imagination part always sounds exciting and enticing, but the warrior part is where the discipline comes in. Unfortunately, there is not much interest among people in the world to venture forth with imagination and courage. Most people are content to follow the crowd and walk the well-trodden path of conformity. But a few people are born Imagination Warriors. Such individuals develop and fulfill themselves through adventure and use of their imagination and creativity. While investigating these ways, Philomena, Daisy, and I passed through a time-space portal to another realm, created when an unfinished painting of a young princess I was working on began to change all by itself. We've found out that an artist named Temporani has also created paintings that are portals to other realms. We have reason to believe that this Mr. Temporani was probably born during the Renaissance, and this little painting we are carrying is one of his creations." Noshi looked to see Marco's reaction to all of this.

"I'm beginning to think this is way above my pay grade, Noshi. It's all so fantastical, and yet here we are marooned on this water world and entrusting our fates to this painting whose colors are beginning to run in the rain," said Marco.

Noshi replied, "Brother, my pay grade's not much higher than yours, but I'm cultivating a theory about this picture."

A mist began to fall as Noshi glanced skyward for inspiration and answers. He looked again at Temporani's painting, and his eyes widened as he saw a detail he had not discovered previously, possibly because it had been hidden under the outer layer of blue paint that represented the sky, now washed away. It was the figure of a girl, painted over with the blue sky above the temple. Under the running blue paint was a simple pencil drawing.

Noshi knew exactly what it was and, reflecting on his insight, thought to himself, "Temporani made a mistake there and probably decided later that he didn't want a young girl flying above his temple. But now I understand something: Temporani imagined a young girl flying, and I imagined a young princess of regal bearing. So our paintings, though separated by centuries, are sisters in spirit."

Marco, seeing that Noshi was lost in thought, remained silent for a while. Then he asked, wincing with pain, "Can you help me up on the wing?"

Noshi gently lifted Marco on top of the wing, and they entered the plane through the only open door of the old jet's fuselage. Noshi was surprised to see that the dark interior was a shell with virtually nothing inside, as if its creator had only been able to imagine the outside of the old Comet.

"I've been holed up here for about a week. I found it on one of my explorations in the rowboat," Marco said. "With all this rain, high tides, and unpredictable whirlpools, I needed a place to relax for a while."

Noticing that Marco seemed to be in quite a lot of pain, Noshi asked sympathetically, "How bad is your leg?"

"The dampness makes it worse," Marco replied. "I remember the last time I saw Philomena. She was preparing to go on one of her explorations of Lamy. She has a deliberate way of cinching up her backpack and setting her canvas sun hat at just the right angle. I miss her so much."

Noshi asked, "How did you find this rowboat?"

Marco began to perk up a bit, smiled faintly, and replied, "After I fell off the wing onto the hard sand, I figured I was a goner. For some inexplicable reason, a happy memory from my childhood surfaced—going with my dad down to a local lake and getting in his row-boat. It was a leaky old thing, but I thought it was the most beautiful boat in the world because it was a place where we always went to be together. I was in such pain after the fall that my body needed rest, and I fell asleep. When I woke up, this boat was resting on the wing of the plane! It seems imagination is a powerful force."

Noshi asked, "Any idea who created the de Havilland Comet we're in?"

Marco shook his head and answered, "No idea, but it seems that if someone's dream or memory is powerful enough imagination does the rest."

Noshi smiled, nodded in agreement, and said, "I know for a fact that your intrepid daughter loves you more than life itself and would do anything to be reunited with her family. Maybe that's all we'll need to return home. I've been working on trying to make sense of all that has happened to us since we entered various portal paint-ings and transited to different realities and times. Here's my theory: Linear time is a fallacy; everyone has the innate ability to create new realities simply by imagin-ing them at the speed of thought." Noshi teared up then added, "We are probably given only a handful of memo-ries in our lifetimes that burn brightly and vividly enough to become the precious touchstones that inform who we are, who we will be, and how we live. We must treasure these always. Your daughter Philomena knows this; now you must see this as well."

Noshi instinctively looked down at his little painting and noticed that the light beams had begun to fade. "We have to move fast now," he said with urgency. "The constant rain is washing away the paint, and I don't know how much time we have. We must get back in your boat with this painting and search for your daughter and her cat."

"What power does this faded painting hold?" asked Marco.

"It can find them. We're going to use what's left of the painting's light beam to direct us to Philomena and Daisy. If they're on this world, we're going to find them," Noshi said, with focused intention.

They jumped down to the rowboat floating under the uplifted wing, offering protection from the rain. Noshi helped Marco into the boat and let out a little sigh of relief when he saw the rain let up a bit. Marco stretched his broken leg out straight in the boat as Noshi began to row away from the old jet.

Philomena, Grady, and Daisy sat on the wet, craggy, black rock watching the tides, monitoring when they could run on the wet sand. They had resolved to leave the relative safety of the old plane in search of answers, Grady jogging with Daisy in his arms because treacherous whirlpools could pop up anywhere. Philomena knew that the constant thunder, lightning, rain, fog, deadly whirlpools, and ground tremors were all signs this world was coming apart. They realized that their goal now was to find a place where they could send out some kind of signal for help and hope for a rescue. On the rare occasion when the fog cleared enough to see their surroundings, it only confirmed their worst suspicions—that this was a lost world of water, an endless ocean that moved with equally endless tides, hidden by its constant companion: the fog.

Philomena looked at the steel gray sky and the featureless ocean and said, "Remember the mural in the temple foretelling a time of challenge and tribulation for the throne-chair people involving water? Well, here we are, wet time-and-space travelers seeking our throne-chairs. But just how much tribulation are we supposed to endure? I've heard of character-building challenges, but this is ridiculous! I'm tired of being independent and strong. I want it all to get easier. I want to see my daddy! I don't need to prove anything to anybody anymore. I know I'm strong, but sometimes a kid just needs a parent to lean on when things get tough!"

Daisy felt her friend's frustrations and immediately replied, "Do you remember when Noshi guided us to the top of his mountain at sunset?"

Philomena wiped a tear from her eye and answered, "Seems like a long time ago."

"What if we have the power to summon the stars and see them fall?" Daisy asked.

Grady, who was aimlessly throwing rocks into the foggy ocean while listening to his fellow castaways, said, "What the heck are you guys jawing about? Sounds like airy-fairy, palm-up stuff," he proclaimed. "We're stuck here, and we're not going anywhere anytime soon. Just my two cents."

"Grady, you're just depressed. You don't like your life, but it doesn't have to be that way. Remember, you created that airplane back there," Philomena insisted as she placed her hands on her hips and glared at him.

"Easy for you to say. You are the unofficial mayor of Lamy. Everyone loves you and wants to please you and be around you, like my sister Mac," Grady replied.

Feeling the need to referee, Daisy said, "Whether you two realize it or not, you have much more in common than you know. You both have aching holes in your lives. Grady, you'd love to have a loving connection with your parents, who are away much of the time, and you've expressed a desire for a bigger, more exciting life. And you, Philomena, long for more time and adventures with your daddy, who is also away much of the time. You need to just be a little girl sometimes and surrender to your wonderful childhood. You guys are tough, strong independent souls, so let's solve this world riddle together. We are running out of options, and we don't have time to argue with one another other. We need to stick together. Form a circle right now!"

"Whoa, I think your New York City attitude is finally coming out!" Grady said, smiling wryly.

The tide was rising quickly and slapping against the craggy rock on which they were sitting. Daisy looked intently into Philomena and Grady's eyes and said, "If there is a chance that anyone else is lost on this water world, we must reach out now."

Philomena looked into Grady's eyes with a stern expression. She held her hand out to him and pulled him down to a seated position.

"Okay, I get it. We'll do this together," he said in a resigned voice.

Daisy glanced at the sky, which had turned a foreboding charcoal gray, with heavy fog now clinging oppressively to the water's surface. She composed herself, looked at Philomena, and whispered, "We must focus our intention like we did on Noshi's mountain at sunset my second night in Lamy."

Philomena nodded, still holding Grady's hand. "Just follow us," she said. "You'll get the hang of it."

"Tide's coming in again. It seems to be stronger every day," Marco said as Noshi rowed against the current. "The fog's been so heavy lately, it would be difficult to explore even If I had two good legs."

Noshi handed the painting to Marco so he could direct its light while he rowed.

Marco winced as a wave sloshed over the boat and hit his broken leg. "The one thing that has sustained me is wanting to be with my daughter again, exploring with her and discovering new things in the earth," he confessed.

Eyeing the dismal, cloudy sky as he rowed against the strong current coming toward them, Noshi looked for a sign that would offer hope, aware that the painting was losing its precious pigment.

Grady gripped Philomena's hand tightly and looked up. Tears welled up in his eyes. Something inexplicable and foreign to him was speaking to his soul as he sat in the circle with his friends, feeling a growing connection to Philomena and Daisy. "I've never before felt that I was part of a team, but now I do and I like it!" he confessed.

Far above them the night fog disappeared, revealing a lapis-colored night sky illuminated with the fiery light of a billion stars. Transfixed by the beauty of their light, the three friends became aware of one particular star whose intense white light seemed brighter than the rest, as though demanding attention. Suddenly, Daisy shouted, "Its descending and moving toward us!"

Grady closed his eyes but sensed it growing stronger and stronger. Philomena looked to Daisy with concern and said, "There is a humming sound, and the air is crackling. It feels electrified!"

Trying to make sense of what was happening, Daisy looked directly at the white light. "Something's in there!" she shouted.

Philomena held Daisy close to her chest protectively as the light became so blinding that they both were forced to close their eyes. Then the humming and crackling sound grew louder and the light diminished. As their curiosity got the better of them, Philomena and Daisy opened their eyes and saw a young woman descending toward them—first her bare feet, then her flowing white dress. "She's not much older than you, Philomena," declared Daisy.

Philomena stared at a young woman not much taller than her, wearing a necklace of opalescent pearls and a crown of fine feathers. Yet what was most striking about her appearance were her gold-flecked brown eyes.

The young woman said to them, "My guidance informs that we must leave now. There are forces that wish you harm, and they will be arriving soon."

Looking at the young woman with the feathers and pearls, Daisy had the strangest sense of déjà vu. "You're from Noshi's painting, through which we first transited!" she shouted in revelation.

Philomena found the young woman's gaze hypnotic. "What is your name?" Philomena asked.

The girl responded, in an equally hypnotic voice, "It is Waya." Then she asked, "Who is in possession of the painting?"

Philomena replied, "The painting is with our friend and your creator, the artist Noshi. We were separated from him and don't know if he is here on this world."

"The painting is crucial, for it is our vehicle to return you all to the point of origin at the designated time," Waya said in a monotone voice.

Daisy's fur tingled, and she asked, "What is the point of origin?"

Waya surveyed the horizon warily and answered, "The temple in New Mexico is the point of origin. It is the dwelling of the first dreamer, the man known to you as Temporani."

"We've already been there, but we arrived about seventy-five years too soon—in the 1930s, by the look of the cars outside," said an exasperated Philomena.

Waya's intense eyes looked skyward from horizon to horizon, searching for something. Then she said gravely, "Temporani knows nothing. He is an old feeble man wandering from here to there endlessly and aimlessly. The painting he created, thought to be a mistake, has transcended its creator, as I have transcended my creator, the one known to you as Noshi. I cannot explain the alchemy that animates us, but my intention is to survive, and thrive in this new realm. This I know: the golden rays that come forth from the temple's doorway act as a beacon in time and space, and that is how I found you. There will be a gathering of twelve souls convening soon, and it is my mission to deliver you all safely and swiftly to the building you know as the Scottish Rite Temple in Santa Fe."

"What is the purpose of this gathering, Waya?" asked Daisy.

After again scanning the skies as if looking for something, Waya said urgently, "Those of us who are fully awakened souls are in mortal danger. We cannot stay here much longer. It is not safe. I am tasked with finding the others as well."

Philomena exclaimed excitedly, "Are you looking for your creator Noshi? Is he here now on this world?"

Waya did not answer but instead quickly raised her slender arms above her crown of feathers.

Daisy felt the air grow dry and begin to crackle again. Waya's feathers seemed to glow as the air around them vibrated. Grady was trying to process their new and unexpected reality. He felt intimidated by this being, regardless of her origin as a painting, and shouted over the sounds, "What will happen when these people—or souls, as you say—gather?"

His question went unanswered, and in an instant they were all flying above the water and looking down at the black volcanic rock that had been their salvation from the rising tide. Philomena, Daisy, and Grady were being supported by some kind of force that Waya was generating as she climbed higher to survey the cloudy water world below. For the first time since they had arrived on this world, they gained a fuller understanding of their environment.

Grady watched in horror as giant whirlpools swirled below, appearing and then disappearing. He noted that they were moving swiftly, at the speed at which the low-hanging clouds were flying by. He thought to himself, "Maybe dreams do come true. Here I am sailing above the turmoil below, finally free."

Waya was now descending, scanning the ocean waves. Watching her as they were flying, Daisy sensed that Waya was expending a great deal of energy keeping them aloft. "Are you all right, Waya?" Daisy asked, concerned. Daisy thought to herself, "She may be a super being, but she's still a girl."

Waya replied, "It is imperative that we find my creator and the painting soon." Looking down, she saw a large form lying in the water and flew closer to it. Daisy noted that Waya's flight had become somewhat erratic as they drew perilously close to the water's surface.

"There, over there!" Philomena shouted.

"It's the airplane!" shouted Grady.

Waya hovered above the airplane's wing and then touched down on its surface. "What can we do to help you, Waya?" asked Philomena.

"I will recover, but I need to conserve my energy for the long return," she replied with labored breath. "My creator is not here, so we must continue."

Waya was summoning the energy to take flight again with her three travelers when the airplane wing suddenly and violently began to sink into the water. "Whirlpool!" shouted Daisy.

The humming and crackling in the air became deafening as Waya lifted off with great effort just before the airplane wing became completely submerged under the waves. Daisy began focusing her powers on Waya and her mission, repeating silently, "Give this girl the strength and power necessary to save us all."

Philomena, Daisy, and Grady all felt Waya's hold on them loosen as she weakened. Philomena grasped Grady's arm as he began to slip through whatever force field Waya had created for them. With one arm holding Daisy and the other gripping Grady's arm tightly, they continued their flight above the treacherous seascape below. Waya was flying just below the low-hanging clouds, scanning the horizons looking desperately for Noshi and the painting.

"There, to the right—that glowing thing! Waya, please descend," Philomena commanded.

Waya swooped down from about eight hundred feet in the air.

"Look, there are two people in the rowboat!" Philomena shouted. The humming and crackling was deafening as Waya continued to descend, containing them in her force field.

"You hear that sound? It's getting louder," said Noshi, searching the skies.

Marco felt the painting move, as though a powerful gyroscope was pulling it skyward, casting its light directly overhead.

"The air is changing," said Noshi.

Marco felt the air crackle and hum. "Agreed, maybe this picture is finally going to deliver," he said with hope.

Noshi stopped rowing and waited in silence, looking skyward as the painting scanned the low clouds that hovered above them.

Marco felt the painting lock onto something in the sky. "Look, the painting is changing! Those little stars at the top are getting brighter!" he said in amazement.

Above them, the humming became deafening and the air very dry. Marco was spellbound as he witnessed the clouds part and reveal the bare legs of a girl. "Daddy, Noshi! It's me, Philomena!" she shouted with joy.

Upon seeing Philomena's father, Grady said cynically, "Your dad must shop at the same clothing store you do."

Noshi was amazed as he saw his painting of the young princess holding his fellow Imagination Warriors come to life.

Waya stared down at her creator with her hypnotic gold-flecked brown eyes as she released her charges into the rowboat. Then she continued to hover just above them.

Philomena fell into Marco's arms, crying tears of joy. "You would have been proud of me, Daddy," she said over the humming.

Marco stood up with difficulty, handed the painting to Noshi, and gave his daughter a bear hug and kiss then said, "I was already proud of you, sweetheart."

Daisy watched as Noshi, his painting, and Waya created a kind of electric bond, realizing something miraculous was happening. "There seems to be a kind of dialogue between the painting's twelve little stars and Waya's feathers," she thought. Daisy noticed that Waya appeared to be getting energy from the painting.

Waya lowered her body so that it was at eye level with Noshi and said, "My creator, we must flee this world immediately. The painting's stars have linked to Temporani's dwelling now. In the center of the temple is a mural."

"The giant painting with the chairs and stars above them?" Noshi asked. Waya nodded solemnly.

Noshi looked deep into her golden-brown eyes and asked the question to which everyone wanted an answer: "How are you standing before us now?"

As the healing energy of the painting infused her entire body, Waya replied with conviction and feeling, "I am your creation, and you are my savior. I will now be your savior. When you three first pierced the veil of the continuum, I was beginning to self-animate."

Daisy asked, "You mean when we jumped into Noshi's painting?"

Waya nodded and said, "Though I cannot explain why I was chosen to awaken from your art, my creator, this

I know: we will all have important roles to play upon our return to the temple. The throne-chairs await us, and critical decisions must be made under the canopy of the twelve stars." She paused as though she were summoning all her energies, and then solemnly looked at each marooned traveler standing in the little boat with threatening whirlpools all around them. While lightning arched across the sky above them as if to punctuate their grave circumstance, Waya continued, "We are all considered transgressors now because of our willful and flagrant violations into the time-space continuum." Waya's eyes narrowed and grew fierce again as she said, "I have recently become aware of powerful forces arrayed against us."

Daisy asked, "Who are these people, and why do they wish us harm?"

Waya replied, "I know them as the Council of Four, but there may be more of them. We threaten the council's status quo in a way that Temporani never did. I suspect Temporani has kept a low profile all these centuries and has mostly stayed in the Council of Four's good graces. This Council of Four has been observing our travels through the continuum, and its members are feeling increasingly threatened by our movements and choices. They've been around since the beginning of time and have had ironclad control of the flow of time. From their perspective, we present a vexing problem. We have unlocked the vast power of our imaginations, and in so doing we have unleashed upon their continuum random acts of nonlinear time. They now understand that by simply imagining, we are able to freely travel through time and space and have the power to control our universe with our thoughts."

Daisy asked, "Why do they feel threatened if just a few more people have the power they have?"

Waya smiled knowingly and responded, "The members of this ancient council have been the time gatekeepers since time immemorial, and they would never give up control willingly. Time is theirs to play and tinker with. You have wrested some control from them, and they are not happy. The high desert of New Mexico will be our base of operation for the resistance. As you know, extraordinary temporal anomalies exist in the village of Lamy, New Mexico. There are also others who have been enlightened, and they will join us in the Scottish Rite Temple in Santa Fe. We are the first of our kind to begin fully awakening. Temporani, during all his travels into the continuum, never became entirely transformed by his experiences." Waya paused for emphasis then, gazing at Daisy, said, "And now I speak directly to you, Daisy. You will soon awaken in extraordinary ways. Are you prepared to transcend your feline body and join your sisters and brothers in the just cause of Resistors of the Council?"

"Waya, what do you mean by transcend?" Daisy asked, tentatively.

Waya smiled at Daisy and said, "When you take your rightful place among the other elevated eleven in your throne-chairs, you will no longer be a cat. Though all your lives thus far have been lived as cat, upon ascending to

your throne-chair in the temple you will incarnate as a nine-year-old girl and truly be Philomena's sister." Daisy's fur tingled as she attempted to grasp the implications of this.

What an improbable sight they all were. Five lost but not yet truly found beings on the precipice of great personal changes and tumultuous times all bonded in spirit and mission, comically crowded into a rowboat floating on an unstable and dying sea, overseen by their savior, the young awakened princess hovering above them. The air crackled with electricity, their bodies vibrated to the alien song of Waya's humming body, and then they were gone.

From their impossibly high and rarefied perch, the council focused their omniscient gaze on the wayward travelers far below them. Two of Four disdainfully muttered, "We'll need to keep an eye on those outliers. They're making a nasty habit of temporally disrupting our continuum." One of Four stated incredulously, "I would not have thought it possible; the mathematical odds of this happening are staggering! A little mistake of a painting, a throwaway sketch, random unintentionality—or was it?" Three of Four, as was her inclination, patiently listened and waited before finally communicating her thoughts to the council, saying, "They are clever, resourceful, and quite ambitious. I foresee some interesting challenges for the council as they grow in number and become stronger and more aware, so it is imperative that we gain control of that wretched little painting. Admittedly, they are also quite entertaining, but we may need to intercede forcefully should they trigger any more temporal paradoxes of the continuum. If they continue to awaken fully, we will all be in great jeopardy." She ruminated further on the outliers' transgressions then proclaimed to the others, "For now, we will watch and wait, but be prepared to act. When is the gathering scheduled?"

## About the Author

Marc Romanelli, a professional photographer and cine-matographer, has photographed in Africa, Australia, Indonesia, New Zealand, Mexico, Europe, and India. He has had a lifelong fascination with the concept of time travel and portals for accessing alternate realities. He resides with his muses—his wife Ahdina and their two children, Philomena and Redford—in the village of Lamy, New Mexico. This is his first book.

## About the Illustrator

Odessa Sawyer, an illustrator and doll maker, works mainly in digital mixed media. Her artwork has graced the book covers of Random House, Simon & Schuster, Scholastic, and other top publishers. She has appeared in *Lürzer's Archive* as one of the two hundred best illustrators worldwide for 2011 and 2014. She resides in Santa Fe, New Mexico, with her husband and son.